Earthworks

"You are sick, friend," he said. "You've been babbling! Unlatch your face-plate and let's have a look at you. You're a landsman, aren't you?"

"I've got to get back to the village," I said. "I'll be late. You know what that means – either the cells or the Gas House!"

"You'd be better advised to stay with us," he said.

One of the women said: "We can't afford to let him go now we've got him, Jess. He might tell the guards on us. He's a Traveller now."

Jess! This was Jess! Throughout the prison villages, that was the name they spoke when they spoke of the Travellers. To landsmen it meant hope, to overseers fear. I knew his life was a legend and there was a reward on his head.

Jess said to me: "We were all landsmen once, convicts sentenced to work on the land, as you are. We have escaped. We broke free and now we obey no order but our own. Will you join us?"

Brian Aldiss

EARTHWORKS

A Methuen Paperback

While life reached evilly through empty faces
While space flowed slowly o'er idle bodies
And stars flowed evilly upon vast men
No passion smiled . . .

RCA 301 COMPUTER

A Methuen Paperback

EARTHWORKS

First published in Great Britain 1965
by Faber & Faber Ltd
This edition published 1988
by Methuen London Ltd
A Division of OPG Services Limited
Michelin House, 81 Fulham Road, London SW3 6RB
Copyright © Brian W. Aldiss 1965

Printed and bound in Great Britain by
Cox & Wyman Ltd, Reading

British Library Cataloguing in Publication Data

Aldiss, Brian W. (Brian Wilson), *1925–*
Earthworks
I. Title
823'.914[F]

ISBN 0 413 17740 8

CHAPTER ONE

THE dead man drifted along in the breeze. He walked upright on his hind legs like a performing nanny goat, as he had in life, nothing improper, farther beyond the reach of ideology, nationality, hardship, inspiration, than he had ever been in life. A few flies of ripe dimension stayed with him, although he was far from land, travelling light above the surface of the complacent South Atlantic. The tasselled fringe of his white sylk trousers – he had been a rich man, while riches counted – occasionally catching a spray from the waves.

He was coming out from Africa, moving steadily for me.

With the dead I'm on fair terms. Though there is no room for them in the ground any more, as was the old custom, in my head I hold several of them – in my memory, I mean. Mercator is there, and old Thunderpeck, and Jess, who lives on outside my skull as a brave legend, and of course my beloved March Jordill. In this book I'll rebury them.

On the day of this new dead man, things were ill with me. My ship, the *Trieste Star,* was approaching our destination on Africa's Skeleton Coast but, as it happened on the last days of those long voyages, the few human crew had shaken into a sort of jelly of relationships, and we were busy suffocating each other, in love and nerves, in sickness and familiarity. Oh, it's an age ago, and like thinking myself into a coal cellar to go back and describe it now. I suffered from my hallucinations in those days.

My eyes throbbed, my vision was cloudy, my mouth was dry, my tongue was coated. I felt no sympathy when the doctor told me that Alan Bator was confined to his bunk with his allergy.

"I'm so damn tired of that man's allergy, doc," I said, resting my head between my hands. "Why don't you just load him up with anti-histamine and send him back to work?"

"I've loaded him up, but it makes no difference. Come and look at him. He's just not fit to be about."

"Why do these invalids ever go to sea? You say it's the

5

salinity of the ocean he may be allergic to?"

Doctor Thunderpeck spread his hands. "That was my old theory; now I am contemplating something different. I am beginning seriously to think that he may be allergic to antihistamines."

Slowly and heavily, I rose. I would listen no more. The doctor is a strange and fascinating man to look at; he is a small stocky square man; big though his face is, there hardly seems room on it for all his features. Eyebrows, ears, eyes with attendant bags, mouth, nose – perhaps especially that mighty blob of nose – are all of the largest size; and what small facial area is not taken up by these features is covered by an ancient acne like a half-obliterated sculpture on a temple. All the same, I'd seen enough of him at this point to last the whole voyage. Giving him a curt nod, I went below.

Since it was the time for the morning inspection and Thunderpeck never took offence, he tailed along behind me.

His footsteps phased in and out with mine as I took the companion-way stairs down to the lowest deck, to the holds. On each deck, lights blinked on and off at the supervisory switchboard; I would check with the robot deck chief before moving on. Old Thunderpeck would follow behind me, docile as a dog.

"They could have built these ships without noise," he said, in an abstracted way suggesting he expected no answer. "Only the designers thought that the silence might prove unpleasant for the crew."

He got no answer.

We walked between the big holds. The all-clear signal on number three was slow in coming up; I marked down the fact on my scratch pad for attention, and looked in to see that everything was all right.

Number three hold was empty. I always liked the look of an empty hold. All that spare space made me feel good; Thunderpeck was just the other way inclined; it made him, in fact, extremely sick. But I had been conditioned to a bit of space. Doc, before he took this simple job on the *Trieste Star* because he was too old for the hurly-burly of the city, had known only city life. With my long spell of penal servitude on the land, I had grown accustomed to the idea of man-made space. Not that I ever grew nostalgic for the misery of those poison-filled fields: the hold was what I liked, of manageable size, and fairly clean, and under my jurisdiction.

I took care to look round all the hold; I met the Figure down there once, and the pulses still race at the thought of it; you find a pleasure in ignoring the stammer of your pulse, especially on the days when you are feeling not too ill.

"Come out when you're ready," Thunderpeck said from the gangway. He suffers from agoraphobia; that's one of the diseases among many that you are liable to pick up in the terribly crowded cities. The tale went – I never checked on how true it was because I liked the tale so much – that he had once found himself in the middle of an empty hold like number three and had heeled over in a swoon.

As we started down the gangway again, I said: "It's a dirty shame, Doc, all these holds empty, the whole ship obsolescent – beautiful ship, not worth a penny." That was my line; he came back with his.

"That's progress for you, Knowle."

Already this account is getting out of hand. Let's start again. The imprisonment words bring! They get all through you, you live in them and out of them, and they make rings round the universe. I suppose they were invented to be a help. All I can say, I was freer when I was imprisoned on the land. The nip of winter. The heaviness of bed those dark nights, with everything you owned on or round you. The stink of the tractor smoke, almost unseen in the blue dawn compound. It's not the words that don't click with the things, it's more that when you write them down they become a different sort of reality of their own. But who am I to say?

This I'll say. In this thundering year, I must be the only one in this part of the world who is attempting to write down any account of anything.

Now I see why things like writing and civilization, I mean chiefly culture and the limits it imposes, were given up; they were too difficult.

My name is Knowle Noland; at the time I am trying to look back to and write about, I was young, sick, womanless, and captain, as they called it, of the 80,000-ton freighter *Trieste Star*, jewel of the Star Line. At the time I write – my now, though who knows who, where or when *you* may be – I am Noland still, lean of cheek, stiff as a board in the

7

mornings, but reasonably clear of mind, with a loving woman, without kin, proud, diffident – both those I was on the *Trieste Star*, but now there's reasons for them, and I know the reasons. Much I know, and may it help me through this history.

(Sometimes the old books have this sort of editorial aside.)

So Thunderpeck and I were parading through the ship on the day of the dead man, as we did every day, and perhaps I do not have to be too particular in remembering what we said. Mostly, we said the same thing.

"That's progress for you, Knowle," he said. He often said that, I know, for he disliked progress, and anything else he disliked he ascribed to progress. At first, when I had not realized how thorough was his aversion, I thought how penetrating of him this was ; but by this stage of the voyage I had got to think of him as a fool. I mean, when you analyse the idea of progress, it is only what men do generation after generation ; and how can you blame on progress what is man, or blame man if you are one yourself? Which isn't to say that I did not value the doctor's company.

"That's progress for you, Knowle," he said.

You have to say something, make the effort of appearing human, when you are working your way through the entrails of a massive automated ship that can and does stay at sea for two years without needing refuel or refit. We had been nineteen months at sea, calling in at most ports only for a day, begging for cargo.

In the picturesque old days, ports had not been so efficient as they were now. There had been all sorts of regulations, and human dock labour with all their strange cult-like trades unions and the rest of it, and refuelling and all the rest of the paraphernalia that's gone ; and then you could spend up to a week in a port, going ashore and getting drunk and the other things that sailors did. I know about these things ; unlike Doc and the others, I can read. Now: nuclear freighters are island universes, moving on their predestined courses, and the few men needed aboard them come to have minds that run in little worn grooves like machines. No wonder I had migraine coming on.

We took in the engine-room, and on the way up again I looked in at crew's quarters in the fo'c'sle. Sure enough, there was Alan Bator, lying on his bunk and staring moodily at the canvas on the bunk above him. We nodded to each other. Alan looked puffy and ruined; I felt like congratulating him on a good performance. And like screaming. Sometimes I get nerve flutter, though I am not one of these sensitive people.

I left the doctor to minister to Alan and climbed on to the poop. On the way up, the world took on a rich dark brown colour, shot with fancy lights in colours that have no name: colours found in old Celtic manuscripts, or embedded in caves. There are aesthetic consolations in being sick; how many times have I thought of the words of our greatest contemporary thinker, computer-programmer Epkre: "Illness is our century's contribution to the good things of civilization."

In the poop I thought for one dreadful second I saw that Figure. Then the shapes resolved themselves into the partly dismantled framework of the autonavigator. Patiently following its working circuit by circuit was one of the robot repairmen. Sitting supervising him was Abdul Demone, a cartoon scanner fixed over his eyes. He flipped it up and nodded to me.

"Morning, Captain."

A civil, silent little man, Abdul. He was a spastic, and never put his bad foot down off the stool as he spoke to me.

"Can you fix it?" I asked.

"The autonav should be working in a couple of hours."

"It better be. We reach the coast by afternoon."

Again my nerves throbbed and fluttered. On a ship, more strain is placed on a man than in the cities. In the cities everything is arranged so that you can spend your whole life without thought; which is a fine arrangement, for a sick man hardly wants to be troubled with responsibilities. Many a time on shipboard I've longed to cut off the autocaptain and drive the ship on to the rocks, destroy it, destroy everything!

On deck, a cool breeze blew. I looked over the neat but cluttered yards of deck; almost uninhabited the deck looked, and naked under the tropical sun. Di Skumpsby was fighting with someone at the rail.

I gave a convulsive start. There was nobody for him to fight with. Apart from the doctor, my human crew numbered only three – Di, Alan, and Abdul. And I knew the others were below. Again the thought of the Figure crossed my mind; I

9

wondered if I were not undergoing one of my hallucinations. Then I mastered my emotions and went forward to help him.

Di was not fighting. He was trying to pull the other person over the rail. As I got nearer, I saw the face of the stranger. It was black and baggy and its mouth gaped horribly.

"Give me a hand, Cap, the fellow's dead," Di called.

The fellow was certainly dead. He was well dressed, though he was soaked with sea water, and his smell was high. His white sylk trousers clung to him. My dead man had arrived; punctual to the tick of fate, our courses had intersected.

"He came over the water," Di said. "Upright, with a stagger. Like he was walking on top of the waves! Scared me stiff, it did!"

On the man's back was strapped one of the new anti-gravity units, a cumbersome affair almost the size of a refrigerator. Since neither of us knew how to switch it on or off, we had an awkward job pulling the man over the rail. He came at last. Something – perhaps a seagull – had pecked out one of his eyes. He gave me his silent frozen scream and I felt like screaming back.

"Let's get him in Number Two Deckswab Locker," I said. Until we switched the unit off, the corpse would continue to drift. At the time it appeared to be only luck that he had fetched up against the side of the *Trieste Star*; but he had not then set in motion the chain of death that followed his vile presence.

The locker housed one of the automated deck cleaners that were activated every morning at dawn. The machine stood bright and unseeing as we bundled our new-found companion into the locker. As soon as we had him secure, Di turned and ran for the rail, and vomited into the sea. I turned and made my way into my cabin and lay down. My brain felt as if it were throbbing and pulsing like a heart.

There are rational things which can be accepted and rational things which can't. I could accept all the reasons for being on a rotten obsolete ship like the *Trieste Star*; I could not accept the reasons for a dead man coming aboard. I rang for Doctor Thunderpeck.

"Di just told me about the corpse. You lie there and take it quietly, Knowle," he said when he arrived. He started to open his little black bag and bring out some tablets.

10

"I'll give you a sedative."

"Have you got something special to cure dead men? It's bad enough sailing on this stinking ship but to think we're being pursued here across miles of empty ocean by a corpse –"

As I accepted his tablets and a beaker of water, Thunderpeck said gently: "You like it on this ship, Knowle, remember that. Remember what you were before you joined the Travellers, and the penalty for that was death."

"Don't remind me of the Travellers!" That I definitely remember saying, and fairly often, for I was feeling guilty then about what I had done to the other Travellers.

"And in the city – you weren't happy there, were you?"

"Look, I know you're right, but I've told you before I'm cursed. How did that corpse get here to me? Don't tell me that was coincidence."

"I tell you nothing. You can work it out for yourself." Thunderpeck loved to lecture me. "You know the cost of these new anti-gravity units; it's phenomenal. Only a very rich man could afford one. There are few of them in production as yet; they go only to heart cases. A ten-stone man can wear one of these units and adjust it so that he weighs only two stone. It saves the heart pump a lot of work. So we know our friend was rich and suffered from cardiac trouble. Right. Where do such people often live? On the coast, by the sea, for the good of their health. So he died walking along the front – people do, you know. An offshore breeze carried him out to us."

"But we're heading for the Skeleton Coast, Doc, if you remember. Nobody lives along there! – No one in their right mind!"

"All right, Knowle, you know best. Now lie down and get some rest. Your persecution complex is showing."

When he had gone, I lay there in the half-light thinking. I thought about the *Trieste Star*. Certainly it was a refuge to me, more than Thunderpeck knew. It travelled and it was isolated, and that suited me. But all the time, far away on the continents, Thunderpeck's "progress" was hunting it down, numbering its days. When I had signed on a dozen years ago, the ports and cargoes were prosperous; now the situation was different. This wonderful leviathan of metal, almost automatic, nuclear-powered, with a registered tonnage of 81,300

11

tons, a length of 998 feet 3 inches and a beam of 139 feet 1 inch, this super-ship, was obsolescent. Its day was done.

Modern as the *Trieste Star* was, it was old-fashioned and being superseded by super-tonnage hydrofoils or the massive new GEMs which could travel almost anywhere, and saw no difference between land or sea. I hated those metal dough-nuts, riding on their pillar of air. It gave me ironic satisfaction to think that they might in their turn be superseded if the newly invented anti-gravity devices were developed to the point where they could carry heavy loads, and carry them economically.

Because of the hydrofoils and GEMs, we were reduced to calling at dumps like the Skeleton Coast for a load of sand, to carry to a soil manufacturer in Liverpool. The costs of the voyage would barely be covered.

What the soil manufacturer did with the sand when we delivered it was a matter beyond the bounds of our interest. I'm an intelligent and self-educated man, but it was sufficient even for me to know that the sand could be made into a soil good enough at least to raise vegetables fit to feed beef animals on.

"The world's hunger takes many sophisticated forms," March Jordill once told me. We were sorting rags. It was evening; I can remember now how the light was. He spoke to me like an equal. "Even religion has become subordinate to hunger, as everything else has, just as in the under-peopled world of the past the thinking of the west, when it had plenty, was subordinated to plenty. We can see that now, though they couldn't at the time."

Sand! It was a noble trade, carting sand round the world. March Jordill, great philosopher and ragman, would have appreciated my graduation from ragman to sandman. He liked small things. A grain of sand might have interested him. The sand we got off the Skeleton Coast was mainly quartz grains, with gypsum and rock salt also, and traces of rare minerals not worth separating, tourmaline and thorium compounds. But for a slice of luck, the whole world might have been made of sand. I begin to get the feel of this writing. It's just a matter of recalling everything and omitting some things, only you have to get the proportions right.

Perhaps I ought not to omit what I heard a popular speaker

12

say about hunger: "Our hunger is our civilization. We have brought beauty and strength from it." I was nine when he said that, and just out of the orphanage. Hammer and I stood at the back of the crowd. When Hammer heard what the man said, he looked down at his own bulging belly, caused by the sprue, laughed, and hit me and ran off.

All your life comes back to you when you sit and think like this. I can remember – I can *feel* that cheezey bed Hammer and I dossed in, under the table. If I chased the straight line of my thoughts, what a maze I'd write!

Listening to all the tiny noises of the ship, watching colours create themselves in the darkness of my head, my thoughts remained soggy with the complexities of soil manufacture, one of the sciences we heard so much about in the land-starved cities. Soil – dirt – dirty days as a landman on a farm – heavy beds, the Gas House – the poor land – working under the supreme rule of the Farmer. I still had nightmares about the Farmer – he pursued me almost as doggedly as did the Figure!

Old childhood rhyme, learnt in the orphanage, never forgotten, hopping on one leg, counting out who was next to be Wolf:

> *Farmer farmer eat your earth –*
> *Coffin cradle coffin berth*
> *Send us food or send us measles –*
> *You're the – maker – of – dis – eases*

And not only the Farmer, but the man I betrayed when I slipped away – got hauled away, I should say – from the farm to become a Traveller. We will get to that some time. Over and over, my mind roamed back to those times, if not when it was rational, then when it roared up the dark old mountains into nightmare and delusion.

Moved by a compulsion, I rose from the bunk and slipped my feet into my sneakers. Feet, shoe, leg, bunk support, floor, shadows, made a mysterious pattern across my vision. What could I smell? Sometimes it was like onions, sometimes like violets. I seemed to remember it from a former time.

Outside the cabin, the set was arranged as it ever was: cardboard deck, plastic sea. The sun lit it too badly, like overdone studio-lighting on a film set. Alarmed about it, I addressed myself.

"I'm very near it again. Now I know the whole thing is an illusion. It's a fake and I'm somewhere else – not on a ship at all. The props are wearing thin! The motion of the ship is incorrect, some of the shadows are misplaced. There must be a better world than this! Gradually, I'm working my way through to reality. And in Number Two Deckswab Locker. . . . Is that where the truth lies? Can it be that truth lies?"

I'd forgotten what lay or stood in Number Two Deckswab Locker. Nobody was on deck, nobody walked on the sea. I went over to the locker and opened it.

He was laughing, a laugh more of power than mirth! I saw exactly the way his lips curled back, wrinkling up to bare the enamel of his teeth, the skin of his gums, in a yellow and terrible humour. It was – it was the Farmer!

"Noland, No. 14759180! You knew I was on the ship all the time, didn't you?" he said. I had not remembered he was so large.

A jolly man, the way the fierce are jolly.

"I knew there was something wrong."

"Not exactly wrong, Noland. It's just that you aren't real; you understand that?"

I kept a sailor's knife in my belt; but if I was not real, could I do him any damage?

"You've come because I betrayed Jess, haven't you?"

"And for all your other sins."

Behind the Farmer was not the locker but something else. My eyes refused to tell me what I saw there. It was an emptiness, but a tainted and unlicensed emptiness, as if when you were talking to a friend, you suddenly realized that you could see straight through one of his eyes and out the back of his head. So supposing he was not real?

With the thought, I launched myself forward, pulling out the knife. As we came together, I sank the knife into the Farmer's ribs. That was real enough! But still he smiled, smiled as we fell together and rolled on the ground. Hugging him, intercorpse. But his smile – no, the world was spinning – his smile stank, and where his eyes had been. . . . The peculiar clarity of vision drew me down into little ripe craters, where worms, white and so exquisitely built, threaded themselves through a dirty fabric. At once, I fell through the fabric of consciousness.

When the fabric reknitted itself, I was lying on the deck. Before I opened my eyes, I felt its heat beneath me, and the power of the sun on the back of my neck. I struggled up and opened my eyes. Beside me, yawning horribly in its eternal slumber, was the corpse that Di Skumpsby and I had pushed into the locker, still attached to its anti-gravity unit. I must have switched off the power as I attacked it, believing it to be the Farmer. I thanked my stars that the hallucination had been so brief. Sometimes, when the migraines come on, I go into that underworld of the spirit for hours. I did go. I used to go. Your tenses get confused over so long.

Peering round the green-painted deck equipment, I saw Di Skumpsby up for'ard. He stood by the rail, staring out across the waters. Maybe he was looking out for another corpse to come into his arms.

Ignoring the pulse in my head, I turned to the thing beside me. It looked as if Thunderpeck's diagnosis of the matter was correct ; the man was old and wore a fine ring on one veined hand. His clothes were good. I wondered who he had been, this poor old bundle who had chosen an offshore wind to breathe his last sigh into. Averting my eyes from his face, I slid a hand into his jacket and felt into his inside pocket. There was a wallet there, and a thin bundle of letters, secured together by a rubber band. I transferred them to my pocket.

Under the corpse's right arm, a red knob protruded forward from the anti-gravity unit's casing. I eased this gently upward. A steady hum, almost noiseless beneath the sounds of the ship, came into being ; at the same time, the corpse began to stir and rise. Keeping a firm hold of it, I manoeuvred it back into the locker and shut the door on it. Then I went back to my bunk to look at the letters.

CHAPTER TWO

At chow time, I was still under the spell of the letters. The food was the usual highly flavoured stuff ; the flavour was artificial and the foods were packed with preservatives. Since they had been chemically grown in the first place, the whole meal, like every meal, was artificial, and I swallowed a couple of vitamin pills afterwards, just to humour my metabolism. My metabolism still felt somewhat shaky; despite the sedative Thunderpeck had given me, I had not slept, so engrossed was I in the letters I had found on the dead man.

There were only six of them, six letters and a telegram. They were all from a girl who signed herself Justine. They were love letters.

Well, they weren't entirely love letters. Much of them was taken up with political matters, and about the various nations of Africa. I have never understood any politics, much less the complex African variety. I skipped those bits.

The world and its nations were at peace at that time. Many harsh things could be said against our bleak social system, but to have peace was worth a great deal; that I often said. For some years, we had been hearing about the threat of war among the nations of Africa, the virile young peoples whose technologies often surpassed those of Europe and America; but a strong man, Sayid Abdul el Mahasset, had become President of Africa and temporarily brought about an uneasy peace among the nations under him.

This I mention here because it will be relevant enough later. But at the time of reading those strange letters, I skipped whenever anything about African affairs was mentioned, in my feverish little search for something personal about Justine.

Of course, the letters were far too brief. Two of them covered only a page. They revealed a warm and complex personality – no, not revealed, hinted at. Yet in some sentences I seemed to be so close to Justine. Perhaps this was because the letters, like all the best love letters, were slightly improper, or seemed so to my interpretation.

It took me a long while to decipher them. Obviously, Justine was a rare and cultured person, or she would never have been able to read and write in the first place. I had taught myself as a child, with the help of March Jordill. His teeth clicked, timing the syllables. I had been glad of my ability during those years on the farm, when I came on a cache of antique books. Since then, at sea, there had been no need for literacy beyond the making of simple marks on pads, and there probably was no book within a thousand miles of us; my talent had grown rusty. Now the struggle with the primitive art form made Justine's letters all the more tantalizing.

They were addressed to a man called Peter. "I am perfectly in earnest," she wrote at one point, "and will do what must be done – on that score, my darling, my ability matches yours. You would know that would be my way of yielding to you, as in my heart I really do." Evidently she and Peter belonged to some sort of religion – in the cities, a thousand differing beliefs flourished, many of them little better than superstitions. In the same letter, she said: "Even when we are together, what we believe keeps us separated; yet when we are apart, we are still together! I gather strength from the world's weakness and ask: Which is it sweeter to do for you, Peter, to live for you or to die for you?"

Much of this was obscure. Its very obscurity, the sense of this woman so near but veiled from me, fanned the warmth in me.

I fell to picturing her, and to devouring her with my imagination. Was she dark, fair, plump, thin, how did her lips look? All voluptuous possibilities fled before my inner eye – but nothing remotely as strange and sad as the truth!

I had never known a woman like this. She belonged to a world that I did not; and the sense of doom hanging over her only made her the more attractive. I envied the man Peter. He seemed to occupy an important position in England; what, I could not tell. From one letter, I gathered he was staying in Africa, and that he had a dangerous decision to take. There were mentions of el Mahasset, the President of Africa. Although the political references meant little to me, I realized that Justine and Peter must be still involved in this enterprise they considered secret and important: the most recent letter was dated only two days ago.

"Yes, you are right as ever," one of the letters began precipitately. "We must regard our love only as a tiny thing – merely personal, as you might say. The Cause must be all; I try to say it and remain myself! To save the world we must lose it, but I tell you, sweet dedicated monster, that I cannot save it if I lose you. I have to have your presence as well as your purpose. Surely you can come here without incriminating yourself? I have bought myself a dress to wear for grand dinners! – All black, so it will serve for mourning as well as evening. I look irresistible in it – you will have to come and see if I am lying."

What they did, where they lived, what they looked like, I did not know. I deduced she lived in a hotel, but she never had an address on her paper. I tried a dozen faces on to my imagining of her, tried to conjure the tone of her voice, tried to touch her in that dress "for mourning as well as evening".

At last I fell asleep, the letters rustling with the rise and fall of my chest.

The writing of this gets easier – or I'm glad to reach Justine. (What were those women I took when I was a landsman compared with her? They were gorse bushes you rolled away from as soon as possible.) I can see it is not just the remembering and ordering of the past, but a genuine creation as well, for the truth is this, and *you* – to yourself you must have an identity – you'd better remember this point all the rest of the way, in case I forget to slip in the warning again – I really do not, with the best will in the world, recall for certain how it was back there on that damned ship twenty years ago. Twenty years is too long. I am different, I was different.

But I still remember how that different man felt, reading those letters from Justine. I can hear their pages rustle on my chest, though I was asleep at the time.

After that sleep, my head felt better, perhaps because it was full of the woman Justine. I told myself how foolish I was. But we had been almost continuously at sea for nineteen months, and the dramatic way in which the correspondence had come into my hands made a strong impression on me. The sun was westering over the sea as I climbed to the bridge to inspect the autocaptain, and the heat of the day was done.

Already our speed was being checked. Over the horizon ahead lay broken water and reefs, the outermost fringes that guard the dreary stretch of South-West African coast where Atlantic Ocean meets Namib Desert. I rang through to the poop to see how the repair to the autonavigator was going. Abdul Demone answered in a little while.

"Haven't made much progress, I'm afraid, Captain," he said. His face on the screen was utterly blank; he still wore the cartoon scanner, pushed up on his forehead. "The trouble is the repairman has seized up in the heat and I'm trying to work on him. I'm hoping to get him going at any time."

"God, man, never mind the robot – get on with the navigator yourself. We shall need it in before the watch is out. What are you thinking of? And take that scanner off and get down to some hard work, Demone."

"I've been stuck here all day."

"I don't care where you've been – I'm saying get some results. Which repairman is it out of action?"

"Main Deck."

"Well, get hold of the one on 'A' Deck. You should have reported this trouble before."

"I rang through to the bridge, sir, but nobody was there."

"Yes, well, buckle down to it now, Demone."

I flipped the screen off. The man had me there. I should have been on the bridge, or have got one of the others up on the bridge. As the freighters were growing obsolete, so men were almost obsolete on the automated ships; almost but not quite. The last step in automation had never quite been taken. Everyone had wanted to take it, but some deep thing in the human mentality had kept them back from that final logical step. The amount of work or good that I and my meagre crew did was marginal, and would have been more effectively carried out by cybos and robots. Perhaps there was something too eerie in the thought of those great grey ships sailing the seas and rarely touching land with no human figure standing, however helplessly, at her helm.

So we existed as parasites, impeding rather than helping the working of the ship. This feeling of uselessness was reinforced when we ran into harbour. In the old days – I've read about it – a harbour was a busy place, a dirty place perhaps, but a human one. Now a dock is a big metal mouth. You move into it and are swallowed by machinery. Machines unload you, machines spit out new instructions to you. Machines see that you get swiftly on your way again.

There are few ports now. The big docks handle trade fast (and will do until the trade is no longer there). In the old days, thanks to human muddle and such institutions as trades unions, you lay in dock for a long while and had shore leave before you sailed again. It's different now. The whole uncanny operation of automatic loading and unloading takes only a couple of hours. Then you're off on your eternal exile again, often without having seen a human soul – though you know very well that the country is packed with them. It's a funny thing in my job: you remain perpetually lonely in a world where loneliness is the rarest commodity.

Hunger was the force that stepped up the efficiency of ports, hunger more than automation. But to explain how even countries like America and the States of Europe became so ill-nourished is a more difficult matter.

Often I've tried to puzzle it out, lying on my bunk and talking to Thunderpeck. We're both educated men, but I can read, and have found things from books that he has not. Even so, I cannot imagine how our ancestors were so foolish as to waste their resources the way they did. Of course the whole mentality of the Prodigal Age from the eighteenth century to the twenty-first is foreign to us.

And I used to parrot what March Jordill told me. Perhaps he was right, perhaps he was wrong; but up till that time, he was the only man I had met who stood the chance of being man enough to be either.

"We can't tell what the world used to be like, boy," he said. "But it seems from books that the population rose steeply in the twentieth century. That brought acute crises in famine-struck areas like the East and the Middle East – that's lands on the other side of Africa. They needed a four-fold increase in food production to cope with the extra mouths, and of course it couldn't be done. Water was the limiting factor."

"Do you need water for food?"

"Of course you do – water and food. One day, you may get the chance of seeing ground, then you'll understand. Countries like America and Australia-Zealand overproduced to feed the other parts of the world, but they only got their own lands into a mess by so doing. Once land gets in a state, once it begins to deteriorate, it is hard to reverse the process. Land falls sick just like people – that's the whole tragedy of our time. Then came the big birth pill crisis, when the long-term effects of progestagen made themselves felt, and then the land wars that left the nations of Africa politically in the lead. History's a funny thing, Knowle, and funniest because you

20

always tend to think it's finished, whereas it's always got another kick coming."

Something like that March Jordill said. Through him I came to see why the rulers scrapped history, as best they could. I picked mine up by accident, and it only worried me.

When I turned that reflection over in my mind, I felt sick and sought company. I went down to the ship's recreation room. Thunderpeck was there with Di Skumpsby, playing cybilliards.

I halted a yard away from them when I saw Di's face.

He scowled at my look of horror. "It's just a temporary rash, that's all, and it's not infectious," he said. His face was seething with little scarlet-tipped spots. He hunched up his shoulder, partially to hide it.

"Just a mild dose of corpse allergy," Thunderpeck said. "Di will be right as rain by morning."

"Corpse allergy!" I echoed. And there I had been entangled with the thing. Instinctively I felt my cheeks. As my hand went up, I saw the Figure, standing behind Di and the doctor.

Oh, don't tell me how clever that black-faced entity is! It stood in the far doorway absolutely still, its arms folded on its breast, with its profile to us, yet eyeing me over the sweep of its cheekbone. I said quietly to the two men: "You know we are being watched? That portent of death is with us."

"It's simply a manifestation of guilt," Thunderpeck said, slyly casting a glace over his shoulder. "You feel guilty because you betrayed Jess the Traveller." He's seen that spectre more than once, but always denies he can see it. That is his form of sickness. Even the doctors are ill.

Di saw it. He gave a blood-freezing yell, threw his cue at the Figure and ran after it. It disappeared through the door. Di followed and I followed Di. Thunderpeck followed us, calling us to stop our foolishness. We whooped up the companionway after it.

The Figure led us up on to deck, stepped into the sunlight, and disappeared. Di and I sat on top of the nearest hatch and stared at each other.

"One of these days, he'll get me," I prophesied.

"Nonsense, it's the ship he's after!" Di said. "It's a real sign of ill omen prophesying shipwreck. The ship is haunted."

"You're both talking nonsense," Thunderpeck said. He

seated himself between us, mopped his massive countenance, and said: "You're just bickering over each other's madnesses. Let's agree on this, that we all have our obsessions and some of them take very real form. I can see it's time you had my standard lecture again."

"Not that thing about my deep-seated guilt again," I begged.

"Not that stuff about how I seek father figures," Di said.

"That partly," Thunderpeck said. "Men of all ages have suffered from irrational fears. Sometimes they have even built systems that attempt to rationalize the irrational, and then you have magic. Magic works when it works at all because there exists in everyone's thought a layer where a wish is as good as a deed, where wish is deed. This layer is generally situated pretty deep, but there are times when for one reason or another it rises and becomes more dominant. Sickness is one such time. In sick people, will and deed become hopelessly confused – hence your hallucinations, Knowle.

"Individuals can be sick; so can whole communities. Communities become sick for various reasons, but one frequently found is when nutritional levels are low. Western witchcraft can be tied in with a general over-dependence on the potato, voodoo with a lack of essential salts, the spirit cults of the Solomon Islands with a deficiency of vitamin B, and so on.

"We have the misfortune to live in one of the most undernourished periods in human history. There is a sufficiency of food in bulk, but in content it consists mainly of deadly poisons. When we eat, we take in toxics, and the psyche reacts accordingly."

I meant to hear him out, but I could not help laughing. I turned to Di, who was grinning too.

"He's a wonder, Di! That's what I call a clever man. The food on the *Trieste Tub* is lousy, and Thunderbird builds a big structure out of it. Come off it, Doc; you're madder than we are!"

"Don't tell me that just because the food's bad this old boat isn't haunted!" Di said.

"Hear me out, hear me out," Thunderpeck protested. But Di jumped to his feet, waving his arms in excitement.

"It's that corpse in the starboard locker!" he said. "That's what's plaguing us! Come on, Cap, let's leave the old doctor to his theories and get that bloody corpse over-board!"

He ran down the deck, his speckled cheeks flaming. I followed, excited, yet even then worried – supposing Di changed suddenly into the Figure. But he remained encased in blue tights and white vest, and we made it to the locker in which I had shut the dead man, the corpse who had played postman for me.

"Listen to the old flies buzz in there!" Di cried. He hammered on the door, laughing as he did so. "Come out, come out, whoever you are, you with the holes in your eyes! Time for a swim."

We pulled open the door and the body flubbed out towards us.

"Get this harness off him and pull the anti-gravity set off," I said. "We don't want to lose that."

"No, switch it off and pitch the lot over the side."

"No, save the unit, Di – it's worth something!"

"No, pitch the lot over the side."

We began to struggle, with the body stiff and stupid between us. Thunderpeck came up and added to our troubles. He was all for keeping the body in a deep freeze unit and giving it a decent burning when we got ashore. It was a silly little set-to. We were all over-excited, and the sight of Di's rash-covered face maddened me.

At last I exerted my rank, and got them to switch off the unit and remove it from the body. When out of operation, the mechanism was enormously heavy, and the straps that secured it in place were soaked with sea water and difficult to undo. Eventually we had the job done. I saw the unit had "Made in Nigeria" stamped on it; a lot of advanced research was in progress there. The *Trieste Star* had come from the ship-builders of Port Harcourt.

Di stood back, feeling his face, as Thunderpeck and I took up the body and carried it towards the rail. He made one last protest.

"Over the side with the devil!" I cried. "He means bad luck for us."

We slung him over the rail and let him go. He went swinging down, down into the brown water churning against our sides. Brown! I looked up and saw our position. The sun slanted low over the sea, casting our shadow far out ahead of us across the water. Reefs showed all round us, sometimes raising a tooth above the breaking waves, sometimes submerged in foam. All the ocean was white with foam and brown with sand. Only as I looked aft could I see calm blue water.

"We're going aground!" Thunderpeck cried. His great rococo face twisted as he ran forward, shouting, and climbed the cling-ladder up to the bridge.

"Come down! The autopilot's on! We're okay!" I shouted.

In the old days, this coast had claimed many a sound ship. But the reefs had largely been blasted to make way for the freighters that called increasingly as soil manufactory boomed; and the automatic devices of the ship, with their thousand eyes unsleeping in the hull, sweeping constantly ahead, ensured that no ship ever ran aground these days. For all that, I understood Thunderpeck's panic. It was certainly unnerving suddenly to see the reefs all round us.

His fear calmed me. I was after him, not heeding Di's shouts from behind.

When I got to the bridge, Thunderpeck was bending over the instruments.

"Stand away! I'm in control here!" I told him.

He made no attempt to move. He turned too late as I went at him. He was fooling with the autocaptain. I brought in a bunched right fist straight as a piston into his solar plexus. Groaning, he crumpled and fell on to his knees.

At once I was sorry. Old Thunderpeck was my friend. But the controls were mine, my pets, the tokens that I was a man with a function. I started to tell him that, shouting to make him hear over his noises. He was bellowing angrily for breath. Red in the face, he looked up and said something I couldn't hear. The intercom buzzed.

"Captain," I said in it.

"Abdul, Cap. Di's here. Say, did Doc tell you – we're fitting the navigator back on, so I switched off the autocaptain while we were doing it to avoid overload. Doc said that we –"

"You switched the autocaptain off – my God!"

Then I understood why Thunderpeck had suddenly meddled with the controls. They'd been looking after things while

I was sleeping and had not thought to fill me in on details.
... And had forgotten some of the details themselves....

I looked for'ard. The water ahead of us was combed with
white. There was no sign of a safe passage. On the horizon
was a smudge that might have been land or a protruding reef.
There was one thing only to be done – close off power and then
take a course slow astern, working on manual.

Before I could lay a finger on the control board, a low
grinding welled up from within the ship. The deck trembled
beneath my feet. We had grazed a reef!

Already it was too late to think of retreat.

There is another thing that has only just occurred to me.
I did indeed spend years feeling guilty at my betrayal of Jess
the Traveller, and as a kid I was long enough bothered with
the thought that I ought to have done something, anything,
to save March Jordill. Yet old Thunderpeck suffered more
then either of them, I would guess, on my account, and I never
worried for a moment about what happened to him. Avoid
it as you will, there must be something special about a man like
me: I don't mean just that I can read and write so well, but
that I ruined the lives of so many persons near to me.

The urge of destruction must always have been in me. If
so, it never burnt brighter than when the *Trieste Star* scraped
that reef off the African shore.

This was the coast of ill legend. I knew what a legion of
ships and men had perished here. Many had struck the reefs
and broken up, while their crews were unable to make the
hazardous passage to shore. I acted almost without another
thought.

I pulled the manual hard over to Full Speed Ahead.

They were great old ships, the nuclear freighters of the Star
Line! You can't tell me that the GEMs will ever mean the
same to a man. The *Trieste Star* responded at once to her
controls. The sea churned and we thrust forward. That deep
discontented rumble slid along the ship and died away.

Lights and alarms lit on the control boards. The double
hull had been pierced in two places, along number six and
seven holds and in number three. I had a momentary picture
of the angry waters pouring in. I closed the watertight doors
in the third hold; holds six and seven contained ballast, and the
doors would not shut. The pumps had come on automatically,

25

but the relevant dials showed that they were not keeping the level of the water down.

I stared ahead. Thunderpeck was picking himself up from the deck now; I brushed him aside. There looked to be a narrow channel ahead, between clearly defined bars of rock. I clutched at the manual, tipping it gently, guiding us through. Already we were picking up speed; in our half-empty condition, we were capable of making 38½ knots.

Exhilaration filled me like the wind in sails.

"We'll drive her to shore if we break her back doing it!" I shouted.

"Slow up while you've got the chance, you crazy loon!" Thunderpeck called. But I was not slowing. Nor was it simply that I felt that here was a case where the safest course was the seemingly wildest one; once I had come to an intellectual decision, madness filled me, the joyous madness of destruction. Under me was one of the world's most expensive pieces of machinery, and I was going to drive it to disaster. The world should see how I cared for its wares!

Perhaps the doctor read something of this in my face. He went and stood at the window, gripping the rail and staring out. The three members of the crew, Di with his mottled face, Abdul limping in his leg iron, Alan clutching a blanket about him, climbed out of the fo'c'sle and stood with their hair streaming in the wind, peering forward in a sort of remote horror.

Once I looked back. Another man stood at a misty wheel behind me, his face dark and veiled, as if yet to be created. It was my *doppelgänger*! The Figure! A thrill of fear took a plunge to my heart. I dared not look back a second time. But the fiery intelligence of those eyes fixed on my shoulder-blades lent extra fuel to my excitement.

At that period I was most sick.

Below the green water ahead, dark shapes lay. We plunged over them. Skumpsby rushed to the rail, peering down, and rock slid beneath our hull. We roared on. Brilliant surf burst ahead. I set her to port, and the wake foamed out behind us as we made towards a break in the line of waves. An alarm bell began to shrill. I cut it dead.

Land was visible on the horizon now, the yellow land and brown that forms this most inhospital corner of Africa. Ahead

26

to starboard I glimpsed a tower, but did not dare to look again. I held to the manual and willed the ship forward to destruction with all my being. Justine, you should have been with us!

Ahead of us, plunging over the waves, flew the dark wing of our shadow. I felt another wing above us. We travelled in the shadow of greater powers than we knew. We are bound to achieve what self-knowledge we can ; it is a point of honour, of intelligence, of courage ; but always in the rambling house of our understanding is one chamber unexplored, one undiscovered stairway leading straight down to the infernal regions. From there came the dark powers and sped with us!

The break in the waves ahead was narrower than I had judged. I saw the water slice across serrated teeth of coral, and I yelled at the full extent of my lungs. We ploughed through with enormous noise.

A terrible sight! Curling up over the side of the ship, a great ribbon of metal! The wrench flung me off my feet. I climbed back to the manual. Thunderpeck sprawled on the deck. Outside, the three crew had been flung down.

The reef had slit us open as if the hull were tinfoil! And I laughed.

We were through the danger for the moment, and with the twin screws still unharmed. The madness was in my head as I pressed for still more power. I cut in the alarms again and let them all ring for the sheer joy of it. We were developing a list to port, the side on which we had been raked open.

Almost I was beyond reading the dials, but I saw now that we headed for shallow water. We were through the reefs – there was nothing but the beach, swinging up ahead. I cut power. We dived on with no appreciable loss of speed. I pulled down the siren and let her blast, as the steam from the overdriven turbines came out on the note of "A".

Alan Bator was running across the deck. He climbed the rail, leapt forward awkwardly, and dived down into the sea. I cheered as he went. His head swept astern.

The list to port became more noticeable ; we were letting in water fast. The white beach loomed ahead like a solid breaker. Beyond it I could see dunes, stony and unwelcoming, stretching into the heart of the land. Coming off it was the hot breath of Africa.

"Ahhhhh!" I yelled.

We struck.

Under the sand there must have been coral or rock. I had not expected such a jar – had, in my exhilaration, expected nothing. I clutched madly at the manual as the ship seemed to fold up round me.

CHAPTER THREE

DOCTOR THUNDERPECK, Abdul Demone and I launched one of the inflatable boats and climbed down on to it. There was no sign of Di Skumpsby, nor did we ever discover what happened to him. He must have been flung overboard and drowned when we struck.

We carried provisions and piled them about us on the little raft. Underneath us, the green water heaved like a giant sleeping. And I was still full of a sort of sick pleasure ; for the whole adventure was real, not an illusion. To that I added a rider: whatever reality was, this was it ; I did not deny that there might be a greater reality, to which life itself was a fake, a shadow show for creatures beyond our imagining.

Straining towards the shore, I had a sensation then – and I call it sensation rather than reflection because it moved so powerfully through me that my skin tingled – which came back to me more than once in the jumble of crises that followed our setting foot on Africa's shore: and comes back to me now, still strongly. I thought all new experiences were welcome to me less for their own sake than because they gave me an opportunity to work deeper into myself.

Obscurely though forcibly, this struck me as a wrong attitude to life. What if it was wrong? Where would it lead me?

The dark was drawing in, but I overrode the protests of my two companions and insisted that we went ashore. The sun was setting as we lowered ourselves for the last time over the side of the great stranded ship ; twilight settled in as we pulled the raft ashore and looked about us. On one side lay the sea, black though the sound of breakers suggested a liveliness it did not show. On the other side was the desert, beaten and broken. Farther along the coast, where I had glimpsed the tower, a light burned, shimmering in the heat.

"That's the way we go," I said. I was full of power, a leader. "There's civilization down there."

Then reaction swept over me. I pitched face down on to the sand.

When I roused, it was with a warm liquid in my mouth. Someone squatted over me, feeding me soup. A light and a fire burned nearby, turning the rugged terrain of Thunderpeck's face into an alien land.

"You'll be all right," he said. "Just drink this and don't worry."

"Doc, I'm sane, aren't I? My head – I mean, the ship – it is wrecked?"

"Sure, sure. The moon's rising. Can't you see the ship?"

"It wasn't another of my hallucinations?"

He pointed, and there was a mountain of shadow, very near: the *Trieste Star*, wallowing in the shallows. I sighed and drank the soup, unable to speak.

Abdul was suffering from delayed shock. As Thunderpeck attended to him I lay there looking up at the stars, wondering why I had done what I had done? Where did the immense satisfaction I felt come from? We were now exposed to a number of hazards, yet I gloated; why? Everything of the little I possessed was gone now, except for the letters of Justine to Peter, which I kept in an inner pocket; how was it that I felt no regret?

All I could tell myself was that the ship belonged to a company owned by the Farmer. I hated the Farmer, and by wrecking the ship I had, in however small a way, made an impression on his vile life. It was the only way I could strike back for the misery I and hundreds of others had undergone, working as landsman on his farm. And I had a nearer reason, though I hardly cared to face it then: the Farmer knew of my betrayal of Jess.... Well, that's all history now, but lying there on a beach hardly less fertile than the lands the Farmer owned, I allowed myself to drift to sleep recalling my time as a landsman (the current and polite name for criminal).

It may have been that obsolete monster lying in the water that brought me the dreams of the farm. The nuclear freighter was a mighty creation; yet it was doomed. In this respect, it resembled the farm. And there was a much deeper resemblance. About both was a primitive quality, a giant naked force with or in which man cannot live without being changed.

That giant dinosaur lying dead in the shallows I had myself ridden to death. But the life on the farm almost rode me to death.

The fields were all square or oblong, and many miles to a side. Where one or two of them abutted one of the rare roads, there a village was built. I used the old penal terminology – the "villages" were simply work camps to which we returned exhausted in the evening.

Hearing our guards shouting that first evening – still vivid! The loss of grip on life, after the prisons under the city, and now this muddy compound, its layout unknown, its uses unglimpsed, its smells unsmelt before.

"You lot over here, double to it! Look alive if you want to live!"

As we went as the voices ordered, glance backward to the long windowless car that had brought us – hated as it carried us half-suffocated on the journey here, now a splinter of longing at its security as it roars preparatory to going, to grinding through the gates, and down the long road for ever.

Strange enclosures – but improperly enclosed – to keep out the gasses blowing from the land. Shouting and stripping, the old loss of clothes, suffered before ; the smell of nudity. Women in this place, too, looking no better for lacking their clothes. Terrific kick on my ankle, frantic hurry to bundle up clothes. Sick, so sick, yet still embarrassed – keen to see, shy to look. Then all jamming together, and the disgust of touch.

More shouting, but they must do it on purpose, and not for order, for it is too confusing. A guard up on a form hustling us by, hitting a woman over the breast and shoulder, clouting the man behind her who moved as if to her defence. Animal silence from us, as we throw our clothes in to a female guard behind a counter. These guards were often landsmen who had worked their term ; unable to adjust to the life of the cities, they stayed on to serve out their ruptured lives in the village camps.

Naked, now we have nothing, nothing but the sweat and dirt on our bodies. Some horrible emaciation here, the swellings and deformation of avitaminosis, a hundred boils and blemishes, like live things growing on rocks. We plunge under a cold shower sprinkling a narrow and slippery corridor. Fear of water, red puckered elbow digs my blue ribs. The smell of the water, something in it that stings the eyes. An old man with rotting feet slipping, falling hard on his spiny backbone, groaning as we hustle him up. His little white organ, a sea shell. Shouting again, dodging blows into another room.

Again the guards hurry us. A young man with a good chin protests, is struck – they drag him outside, kicking the bare legs that he tried to hook about the doorpost; tremble of sympathetic fear for him, his softness, part-selfish.

An issue of clothes. The uniform. Strange gladness at the blue jacket. We are being given something! Presents from the Farmer. We look at each other, shyly, knowing we will have to know each other, but now only thinking that these are stout good kit, so that something shines in our faces. Isn't giving kindness, even with the kicks? In line, we take the things, secretly agog, jostle together in the little room, and still cowed scramble into blue serge blouse and trousers. No garment has a sex, all are trousers and blouses. We stand there awkwardly, awaiting more shouts, strange in every way. We look at each other, do not dare talk. The guards cluster at the door, chatter together, laugh perfunctorily.

We stood there for a long time. I saw how short the sleeves of my tunic were; a man next to me with a scarlet birthmark over his forehead and eyebrow – Duffy, I knew him as later – had a blouse far too big for him. Our eyes met. Everything was assessed, the profit, the risk. The guards kicked their heels; all government machines work the same way, infinite hustle, infinite delay. I slipped off my blouse.

Slowly, Duffy nodded. His eyes never leaving the guards, he slipped off his blouse. We exchanged garments, a better fit. At once the guards began to bellow.

Again we were on the trot, being allocated our huts. Like cattle, we teemed through the door. In the stream of bodies, I had no time nor space to get the blouse over my right shoulder. As I shot through the doorway, one of the guards landed a terrific blow on that shoulder. I slipped, fell down the two steps outside, carrying another fellow with me. Sharp pain in my leg. The other fellow was up in a flash and off. I took longer. A guard waiting outside roughly swung me round as I came up. My face struck the edge of the open door.

Terrible fury and pain, a high noise in the head. My nose began to bleed. Cupping it, I slobbed forward and along into Dormitory Five of B Block. Miserably, I fell on to the nearest empty bed.

The dormitory guard was there, a permanent man who slept at one end of the hut and was in charge of it. I knew, as I saw segments of him from between bloody parted fingers, that he would be coming to haul me off my bed. In the fury of hurt, I determined to destroy him the very moment he touched me. I jerked my fists from my face and turned to confront him. It was Hammer!

"Boy," March Jordill once said to Hammer, in one of our evening sessions as we sorted rags, "you're an awkward and infernal little cuss, but given the chance you would not have made a bad citizen. That may sound a pretty low level of praise, but it is a stamp you will always bear on you, God knows why, whatever scrapes you get into. No one will ever get any real use out of you, but you'll never make a really successfully bad citizen. They'll hate you for that, so watch it."

But we didn't hate Hammer in Dormitory Five. He still had the negative goodness in him that Jordill had recognized in the little fat lout with the sprue. Much as he swore at us, much as he drove us (and he had to drive us or we would not go), he had compassion, and but for Hammer it is unlikely I would have survived those arduous years. He was rough, foul-mouthed, and a saint. Not that Hammer could do anything to mitigate the crushing crudity of our way of life. Medical treatment was nil, there were no laundry facilities, and I never changed those clothes in which I began my sentence.

"They don't care if you snuff out," Hammer said one night at bunk-time. "The human body provides valuable phosphates for the land. You're worth more dead than alive to them, and look at the precious dirt you carry round with you!"

Certainly it was true that the mechanicals and robots that slaved among us were more valuable than we. Scratched and battered though they were, they worked better than we did. Every landsman made it a point of pride to do his tasks as slowly and badly as it was possible to do without tasting the overseer's whip.

Of all the sad and dehumanized people in our village, I think I was the only one who could read; what a precious thing that archaic art was to me; and I did not let even Hammer know my secret.

We were roused early by sirens and a visit from the overseers, driven to get to our work. The monotony of life! — varied only by the seasons that even the Farmer far away in his city could not abolish.

Those years were made of hardship. Better things also lay among their lost months. A kindness from a fellow could charm your whole day. And in the summer came the sun in strength, to put into limbs a life that in winter they lacked. Also there were the women in the village, with whom we could taste the poor man's traditional pleasure.

Death was there, too, that other great deliverer of man from his monotony. No longer could I laugh at it as I did when Hammer and I were boys, as it showed itself now in true form with which you could never come to terms, a thing of sudden collapses, of sweats, strange noises, vomiting, rolling eyes, and involuntary bowel movements.

For all that, the longer one served in a village, the easier life became. Although the system was not designed to admit trust, the land could not be worked without it, and so gradually one showed one was not just a madman, and a strictly limited measure of freedom was granted; which freedom depended largely on the fact that there was almost nowhere to escape to.

Because nothing but what a man regards as true freedom — whatever that happens to be — is tolerable to him, even the best day was stamped with the monotony of the least, and my last day in the village began just as inauspiciously as all the others.

As I said, we were forced to rise early. Our dormitories were plastic huts arranged about a central mess hall. Round our huts was a fence of barbed wire; beyond that we were surrounded by garages, maintenance sheds, and the administrative block; then there was wire again. All round the squalid little encampment stretched the land.

I left my hut at six-thirty, wearing my landsuit, which was an all-enclosing suit like an asbestos suit: light but air-tight, and with a helmet attached. I kept the face-plate open, since

33

the day looked fresh and the previous day's spraying in this area had been negligible. England on a May morning can feel good, even to a landsman. You remember the winter and are grateful. The whole sky was a bed of little fleecy cirrus clouds – hardly clouds, for the sun shone bright and chill through them. A yellow mist like a coating on a sick tongue lay over the land, a reminder of the spraying for dilly beetle we had given the place two days before. It exuded a scent that stuck slightly in the throat; most men kept their face-plates closed because of it, but I insisted in keeping mine open, fool that I was.

I pushed through the airlock into the messing hall. Everything was very noisy there. People were still dazed with sleep and morning, but they talk as much as they can then because they may not have the chance to speak to another human until evening. At least, that's how it is in summer: in winter when it's dark, they are much more quiet. The mess is like a morgue in January.

One thing I will say for the village. While you live, they expect good work from you, and so you get your regular 20 grammes of animal protein every other day, at supper. In the cities, during the frequent unexplained shortages, you can go weeks sometimes with no meat ration at all. In the orphanage, we were always on half-rations. None of which makes village breakfasts appear better than they are.

After you have eaten the poisonous slop they call porridge, straight round to the overseer to find what job you are given. You are searched and checked before being let through into the outer perimeter. Then round to the garages, since the ideal is to be away before seven. The inspectors and overseers are there to see you move.

This morning, I was told I had a detail some miles away, at a point which I already knew from previous details. It was a fine morning for a drive; I climbed gladly into a tractor and fed it the co-ordinates, and it set out at once.

That brief time alone was worth an extra bowl of soup! Strictly speaking, the camp overseers are meant to ride with you and hand you over to the work-point overseers. But not only are they perpetually short of staff, but the overseers are lazy men, and often as crawling with ills as the landsmen under them. So if they think you are trustworthy and will

34

not try to escape, they send you out alone. They know there's nowhere for you to go; the whole damned island is a sort of prison camp.

Of course, you might always run off and join the Travellers. But officially the Travellers are treated as a superstition, like the crackpot religions that thrive in the camps, for all that officialdom does its best to stamp them out. There have been cases (or so every landsman fervently believes) where Travellers have surrounded villages in strength, burnt them down, hanged all the guards and overseers, and released all the inmates. Myself, I was sceptical; I had never seen a Traveller, and my upbringing taught me not to believe anything I could not shake a fist at.

A light misty rain began to fall as we moved along. In fact this was insecticide, and the sprayers were already circling above the fields, sweeping over the land again and again on their morning flight, and not missing an inch. Being enclosed not only in my suit but in the tractor cab, I was doubly safe. We passed an area where a big machine was jetting out a chlorophyll correctant, sending a dense green mist out to meet the rain of insecticide. The crops there had failed, owing to an outbreak of the so-called topsoil physichosis, they stood there withered and brown, like old men planted after death.

It seemed to me for a while that I was moving over the face of an alien planet. This was not a world that I could know, or that would tolerate me. To have stepped out on to the surface unprotected would have been to suffer a painful death.

At that reflection, a terrible sorrow moved like a worm in my heart. Somehow, I had been dispossessed. Most of the old features of the land had been removed or altered. Small hills had been blasted flat, streams and rivers flowed in straight lines across the landscape. As we climbed up towards a gradual escarpment, I recalled how a line of great trees had grown here a few years ago. Now the wind blew unobstructed, and the shoulder of land lay bare and dismal. Machines brooded there. This was my rendezvous. I went and reported with my work stamp to the foreman overseer.

We worked hard that day! It was complicated and perilous work – and unnecessary, too, if the truth is told.

For on the other side of the escarpment ran a main road,

and on the other side of the main road lay the farm of a different farmer. Our Farmer owned many thousands of square miles of land. How many, I did not know, but it was understood that his territory stretched from the south coast up to the midlands; none of us at the village had any possible way of checking the truth of this. But we did know that this point marked one of the northern limits of his land. It was patrolled by fast automatic things, things that howled, bleeped and chattered to themselves – normally the only live things in the area, except for the traffic that did not stop and was not allowed to stop.

As the other men and I climbed the tall pylons, clamping the mesh to them, the traffic slid beneath us, cars and GEMs making down the road, carrying their passengers sealed safely within them from city to city.

In the city lived the Farmer. We did not know his name; he was too far above us for his name to be known in the village, even to the overseers. In the interests of efficiency, farms had slowly grown bigger and bigger, swallowing the little unproductive units. As the population grew, the farms had to grow. In the interests of the same bleak god Efficiency, the railways had long ago been lopped until they were a skeleton of fast main lines rushing between distant points with unimagined cargoes; their contact with ordinary people grew less and less.

As the population grew, and more land was required for agriculture, the road system underwent the same drastic simplification in the interests of the same alien god. Only a few main roads were allowed; they formed a gird across the land that would not have disgraced an euclidean textbook.

It was not without deliberation that the experts did away with most of the railways and most of the roads; for among the minions of the god Efficiency is one called Centralization. Centralization was well served by the amputation of the transport system. As a result of the amputation, villages and many town began to die. Efficiency was thus increased, Centralization established.

The only urban units now were the giant cities and the meagre villages, which latter in happier eras would have been called labour camps. But in this enlightened age, prisons were done away with, and you served your sentence for the most trivial offence by work on the land; "rustication", they sometimes called it.

Despite all the machinery employed on the land, there was still plenty of work for humans, work often too dangerous for machines. Our work on the pylons was too precarious and difficult for any machine yet invented. The pylons stood along the line of the ridge where the trees I could remember had once grown. We were engaged in stringing a vast metal net between them, from six feet above ground to forty feet above. And as I climbed and clipped and riveted, I cursed the Farmer who sat in his office in the distant city, shuffling his papers and never seeing the sullen ground over which he ruled. At that time, I did not know enough to curse the system that had supplied the man.

Directly below me, the earth was broken and eroded. The infertile subsoil showed through. This was what had happened since shelter and binding provided by the trees were gone. The trees had been cut down to get rid of birds, which were currently being destroyed because of their ability to spread crop disease. Now we were building tree-substitutes; they would act as windbreaks, as the trees had done, and stop the wind from blowing away the soil and exposing more subsoil. Nobody admitted that this showed some sort of basic failure in the system.

As the man below me unrolled the steel mesh and I secured it, we gradually worked higher up the pylon. The nearest city came into view, its serried roofs visible through the mist. It squatted on a giant platform, raised on legs high above the surrounding land where the poisons in the country air could less easily reach its inhabitants.

A pang of homesickness ran through me, although I knew how overcrowded it was in the dark alleys of the metropolis.

Something else I could see from my vantage point. Breasting the road only a short way off lay the ruins of one of the old towns made obsolete when the grid-road system was established. Much of it had been cleared away to provide more arable land; but much remained.

Two years earlier, I had been engaged on that job of clearance myself. A landsman was made to work at anything during the term of his rustication. There in those ruins I had found a secret cache of books, and smuggled some back to the

37

village. They lay hidden under a loose board under my bunk.

I resolved now to visit the ruins and see what else I could find. I hungered to do something forbidden.

We worked through the day, with a break at noon to drink turnip soup from a flying canteen. At dispersal time, when the hooters blew, it was easy for me to drive across to the broken township, since I was the only member of that work detail from our village. None of the work-overseers cared a rap what happened to us after they had given out our work stamps.

I kept under the line of the ridge, out of sight of the things that squarked to each other as they patrolled the road. The ruins were dark, silted up, promising. My tractor bumped over a great pile of rubble in front of them. With a swing of the wheel, I twisted between two houses and under the awning of what had been a shop. I was immediately out of sight of prying eyes.

The time factor was important; they would expect me to check in in the village within a certain time after the hooter, or else I'd be for no supper and the cells. For all that, I sat where I was for a moment, taking in the feel of the kind of place my ancestors – whoever those faceless optimists had been – lived in.

The shop window before which I had stopped was shattered. Through it lay darkness, darkness and mouldering things. The houses were only remains of houses, husks, their core eaten by the elements. Rubble had been bulldozed against them from behind, as high as the upper windows. It could not have been more desolate. The desolation was emphasized by the glimpse of bare tillage and struggling plant life visible between the buildings. Yet I saw here the ghost of a more human order of life, when the mass unit had not been the only standard. Here was the corpse of a world where the individual had had some status.

Clamping down my face-plate, I climbed out of the tractor. Moving fast now, I made my way between the buildings. This had been some sort of central part of the city; I recognized the building from which I had taken the books, without knowing what sort of building it was. In the books themselves I had found possible labels for it: bookstore, library, museum, reading-room; but which it was, or what the differences between the terms implied, I did not know.

The place was more in ruin than ever. The demolishers had broken down all the front of it before the operation was suspended; I climbed in through a back way, into a murky room. My heart beat very fast, my nerves stammered.

Something moved across the window through which I had scrambled. I turned. Two men jumped in and grasped me savagely by the arms. Before I could struggle, a dirty hand clamped over my face-piece and my head was jerked backwards.

They saw the yellow star on the breast of my suit.

"He's only a landsman!" one said.

They let me stand up straight though they still held me tightly.

"Who are you?" I asked.

"We ask the questions here. Get moving, lander. The boss would like to meet you." One of them produced a knife. Taking hold of my suit, he dug the knife into it, and jagged a cut in it about three inches long. I grabbed it in horror, pursing the lips of the gash so that the pure air did not pour out. This was standard procedure for dealing with anyone who looked like making trouble; with a cut in your suit to nurse, you are too busy to do anything else.

The shock threw me straight into an hallucination.

The men took me out of the ruined building to another I had not noticed before. It was miraculously preserved. Inside, it was furnished in the style of an earlier and more luxurious age, with curtains made of natural fabric hanging everywhere, and big dark musical instruments in a corner, and plants not used for eating, real woods, and strange pieces of furniture to sprawl on.

A fat man, such as you rarely see outside hospitals, sat at a table. He was eating ancient kinds of food, brightly coloured, with complicated instruments. When I entered, he pushed them aside. He stood up, and the man brought me over to him.

"You have anything of value?" he asked.

In my pocket, I had a picture of someone. It was someone I had loved, someone who depended on me; either I had let that person down or he or she – I knew not who it was – had let me down; but love was still predominant in the relationship, which continued strongly though it had been severed long ago. This picture was my own, my only, my valued symbol of this person.

I clutched the picture convulsively.

"I have nothing for you," I said.

The fat man sneered. "You must have something, you fool. This is the Twentieth Century, not the Twenty-Second; everyone has possessions still."

The men wrenched my hand out of my pocket. I held the picture clenched in my right fist. They bent my forearm over the edge of the table. One of them brought the side of his palm down with a savage chopping motion. Pain scissored up my arm and shoulder. I cried and the picture fell on to the floor.

The fat man picked it up and walked over to a large tank standing by the window. I ran after him. The tank was full of a liquid with a familiar smell. How often have I not smelt it, in dreams and waking! It was a reinforced chlorinated hydrocarbon called Oxbenzide. We used it diluted to one part in ten thousand of water to kill off the hardiest pests. The fat man tossed my picture into it.

I saw that adored face curl down through the liquid, disappearing, seeming almost to suffer in the tortuous path it took.

I plunged my hand into the liquid to save it.

The beloved picture was almost within my grasp when my arm began to dissolve. A lethal paralysis syphoned up my veins. In the liquid, nothing remained. Straining my mouth open in a sigh of shame and fear, I fell back, clutching my stump of arm. The dissolution was climbing towards my shoulder.

The evil hallucination burst, pitching me – still sobbing as if I would sob for ever – back into the real world.

I lay across a bundle of sacks in a dim-lit ruined room. A group of ragged men looked down at me. So I found myself for the first time in the company of the Travellers.

CHAPTER FOUR

So I have managed to get to the Travellers, after working for two months – or not working, which was as bad – on this manuscript. Perhaps I should have started with them, since they are so important a part of my life; for although I was with them for a short time only, the strangeness of them had terrific force: there was room in their system for trust and charity. And that was so although they were the most hunted of men. More importantly, the Travellers represented some sort of initiative for the future in a continent full of dead ends.

No, I could not start with them. You need courage to write, and courage grows by one's own example more than by the example of others. You need courage because writing is confessing, and my biggest confession of all must come in this section. I loved the Travellers, yet I betrayed Jess! Also, the feel of how writing was has come over me; I have performed a sort of resurrection of this ancient art form. Syntactical arrangements, semantic mechanisms, come to my aid, allow me to convey my thoughts to no one! Or perhaps after this war, the remnants of humanity will rediscover caves and, crawling into them, confine their language again to paper, so coming to learn to read again. (Of course in my heart I have that hope.)

But will they understand? Have I put in too little or too much? Should I have left out the winters in the city, and the idiocy of my arrest, the clearing of snow in the villages, the despair, the knowledge that life always grew worse? Should I have put in my hallucinations, so real at the time and now, after a lapse of years, so repugnant to me, should I fiddle to produce footnotes, aping some of the books I find?

No way of solving these problems exists any more. The conventions collapsed like old bridges. On the one side of the gulf is the mind, eternal and untouched – on the other, the body, running, jumping, bleeding. Better to copy the method of the thrillers I find among old book piles (converted by the passage of two hundred years into the subtlest of all signposts to those old days of plenty), and stick to the body. The mind can take care of itself, as it has had to from the very beginning; it's not as smart as body, but it can survive. And when I cannot resist it, I will pop up and be my own editor and commentator.

With this coaxing, imagine for yourself my feelings: I lay on the sacks looking at those ragged men. Nobody spoke, I could not speak, my brain numbed by the illusion that I had lost my arms. My breath rattled in my throat, changing tempo

41

only when the leader of the Travellers came up to look to me.

The faces of all but him were the faces of men and women of that time: faces lean and dessicated by the effects of constant malnutrition and hardship, faces in which could be read the determination to wrest what little they could from life and the sort of intelligence which hunts under the name of cunning. The women, reduced almost to sexlessness by their rough garments, hardly looked gentler than the men. Though the room was dim, I saw their faces clearly ; the door had been converted into a crude airlock to trap most of the drifting gasses from entering, and few of them wore landsuits.

The leader's face was different from the others. It had acquired in its starved lines an asceticism that transcended hunger. He was instantly marked out, not only as a man who had suffered, for nobody present had escaped that, but as a man whose spirit had transmuted the suffering into something finer. Before setting eyes on him, I had never appreciated the difference between mere endurance and durability. Directly I saw him, although I had never seen such a face before, I knew I could expect mercy at his hands.

He came forward with some sort of an adhesive patch, and with it mended the gash his men had cut in my suit. All the while, he looked penetratingly at me.

"You are sick, friend," he said. "You've been babbling! Unlatch your face-plate and let's have a look at you. You're a landsman, aren't you?"

"I've got to get back to the village," I said. "I'll be late. You know what that means – either the cells or the Gas House!"

"You'd be better advised to stay with us," he said.

One of the women said: "We can't afford to let him go now we've got him, Jess. He might tell the guards on us. He's a Traveller now."

Jess! This was Jess! Throughout the prison villages, that was the name they spoke when they spoke of the Travellers. To landsmen it meant hope, to overseers fear. I knew his life was a legend and there was a reward on his head.

Jess said to me: "We were all landsmen once, convicts sentenced to work on the land, as you are. We have escaped. We broke free and now we obey no order but our own. Will you join us?"

"Where are you escaping to? There's nowhere to go," I said.

"That we will tell you in due time. First we must know if you will join us?"

I looked down at my hands. In fact it was not a question in which I had any freedom to answer as I would; that sort of question was gone from the world; I thought that for my throat's sake there was only one answer I could give; now I knew where they met, I could not be trusted back in a village. "I will join you," I said.

"His tractor will come in handy, any case," one of the men remarked. "We can use that."

"No," Jess said. "They will soon track down a lost machine; men take a deal more hunting, and are less important anyway. What's your name, friend?"

"Knowle Noland."

"You call me Jess – just that. We Travellers form a brotherhood and you'll soon get to know us. What little we have, we share."

"I've heard your name spoken."

"Right, Knowle, go and start up your tractor. Set it going across the farm, so that it heads well away from here, and then jump out and come back to me."

Stiffly, I clamped up my face-plate. They looked at me hungrily and in silence. I could feel their lack of trust. Without a word, I turned and walked out under the wet blankets that formed an airlock at the door. Outside, an early evening calm was falling over the ruined remains of the town. A pair of sentries were snuggled into the rubble; they watched me without speaking.

I picked my way past the place where they had captured me, which was only a few yards away. I came to my tractor, climbed in, started it. Slowly, I backed it from the awning and pointed its nose towards the miles of open field.

What life would be like among the Travellers, except that it would be unimaginably hard, I knew not. Life at the village was something I knew. If I drove back there fast, I might get no worse punishment than a week in the Gas House. The Gas House was the nickname for the factory – one stood outside every village – where the produce of the land went before it was carried away on autotrucks to the city. In the factory, the poisons on which the produce had been nourished, the phosphates, potassiums, magnesiums, and the insecticides and arsenicals with which it had been protected, were sluiced off under heavy sprays. Working those sprays, manipulating the foodstuffs, was not in itself a hard punishment. But every week in that poisonous atmosphere was a year off a man's life. Robots were not allowed in there; they would seize up, and they were too expensive to risk.

Revving the engine, I looked back into the ruins. I saw half a dozen heads, half a dozen rifles. I was being covered. They would shoot if I tried to make a break for the village. Without further thought, I set the tractor in motion, jammed one of my cable tools down against the fuel pedal, and jumped. For a moment I stood there, watching the machine gather speed and head away over the open land, straight through a cabbage crop. Then I turned back to the ruins.

"You're not so clever as I expected," I told Jess. "The trail of that tractor will be easily visible to anyone who cares to investigate."

"We're moving out of here in an hour or two, when it's dusk," he said. "Now come with us and eat. You're a Traveller now."

The soup was vegetable water. The meat was that of a cow they had stolen from a cattle pen some miles away. The beast had been fed on stilbestrol to promote growth; its flesh was pulpy and obviously lacked key nutrients. Stilbestrol itself was known – and had been known for over a couple of centuries – as a carcinogen; but we had no option but to eat it. In the frantic drive to keep food production level with population increase, no pure food, as the ancients would have recognized it, was left on the planet, except perhaps in a few remote corners.

But if the food was bad, I found the company good.

These outcasts now accepted me easily enough as one of them (though I was careful not to let them know I could read print, since I soon discovered that every one of them, even Jess, was illiterate). So I found out something of the way of life of the Travellers.

I cannot say I became one of them. Nor was I with them for long. But that experience was vital, and some of the lessons of survival that I picked up then, with Jess and Garry and

Haagman and the others, have been useful to me recently. And the touch of freedom I experienced – so novel was it that it frightened me at the time; but it has grown in me since.

Almost before the meal was over, the men were putting their kit together, though they had little enough in the way of possessions. They moved out in single file, into the gathering dark. As I got up, Jess detained me.

"I must question you on one thing, Knowle," he said. "Our biggest problem is not the enemy but the disease. Cancerous people we're happy to have, because it isn't infectious, but tuberculous or other diseases we sometimes have to turn away. Now, when you were brought before me, you were plainly in a kind of senseless state, and crying out about losing something and I don't know what. You will have to tell me what it is that ails you."

Letting my head hang, I tried to find myself words. The truth is that I was very ashamed of my ailment.

"If it's some kind of a mental thing, we don't mind that. Most of us are out of our right minds anyhow."

In a low voice, I said: "It was a sort of food poisoning I got as a child in the orphan centre in the city. A doctor said it affected a part of my brain and my retina. He called it a scintillating scotoma, I think, with something else I can't remember. That was why I was arrested and made to serve as a landsman – I had a sort of vision one day when I was in the street, and I walked out into the traffic way and caused a bus to run up on to the pavement. So they sentenced me to the village."

He said gently: "You must become one of us in mind as well as in the flesh. It's your only hope of survival. We have a talent for recognizing those who may betray us. We shall know when you are really a Traveller, heart and soul, and then you may get a woman and we will look after you whatever happens; no true Traveller ever deserts or betrays another."

"You needn't think I would ever betray you! I'm not that kind," I said angrily.

With infinite calm, he looked into my eyes. That lean face seemed keep enough to cut into my inner mind.

"If you are with us long enough, you will grow to know yourself. It is that that makes the desperate life of a Traveller

45

worth living; you can escape the guards, but never yourself. When that day comes, you will see where betrayal lies."

I remembered his words bitterly later, though at the time they meant little to me. This I will say: that in that ragged bunch of desperadoes survived, I do believe, all that was left of the nobler codes of an earlier way of life, debased, trampled by the necessities of life, but still apparent. And Jess kept the spirit alive in the others. Without him, some of them would have been little better than wolves.

Soon it was dark, and we were moving.

I fell in with a man called Garry, a soft-spoken man who rarely smiled. His silence made me welcome. We moved two abreast, the couples spaced apart.

Overhead, a lonely Iron Wing was dusting crops. We paid it no attention. It was robot-controlled and would not see us. We were moving away from the village from which I came. Disquiet rose in me. I longed to get back to that world I knew, to Hammer, to the familiar routine. I did not wish to be a Traveller, to be bound to cross and re-cross for ever the reeking earth without hope or home. But how could I escape from this band?

The Travellers formed a free society within the great prison of England. Because conditions on the farmlands were so inimical to life, only men and women convicted of "crimes" worked there. To keep up the number of land workers, the laws in the great teeming cities had to be made increasingly strict, so that new infringements would maintain a supply of new labour. But some of these labourers escaped from the villages, and formed themselves into bands.

There was no hope of their getting back to their families in the cities. The cities, perching on their high platforms above the land, were impossible to enter illegally, or almost so. So the Travellers travelled, living as free a life as possible within their wide prison, until they were hunted down by machines or dogs or men.

We showed we were free all right. We marched till near morning, and then camped in an old garage, no longer used, on the edge of a main highway. Easy though it was, the pace we had kept almost killed me, for I was unused to their sort of walking. But I saw now why they were legend; they came and went as they pleased, often on regular routes of their own; they migrated and hibernated, they appeared and disappeared.

"Where are we heading?" I asked Garry.

He named the place, without particularizing too much, as if he had not too much faith in me. He told me we were escorting two men who were merely passing through this territory. They had come from the north and would be passed over to another band of Travellers farther south. They were heading for the sea, and hoped eventually to sail to Africa and freedom.

"Aren't we going to the coast?" I asked.

He shook his head. With prompting, he described the shore that I had never seen, and the sea beating endlessly against a margin endlessly bound by concrete and plastic and metal – for the old beaches had all been eaten away in the manufacture of artificial soil.

He snuggled down to sleep. Tired though I was, I remained awake until long after the daylight insinuated itself through a hundred cracks into our shelter.

Over the days that followed, I learnt more about the travelling life. Though I admired it, some sort of fear kept me from feeling myself part of it.

Jess himself never made any attempt to extend his liberty, however much he helped others. He lived his desperate life in the heart of the enemy. The same held for his more faithful followers. Some of the men – now that their faces became individualized and less strange to me, I saw they numbered about twenty-five – told me that it was fairly simple to remain at liberty as long as one kept away from the villages and did not venture on to the roads, all of which were well patrolled by robots.

"Besides, robots are fools," one of the women said. "By relying so heavily on their machines, the Farmers don't realize what liberty they give us."

"But what sort of liberty is it, after all?" the man next to her growled. "The liberty to die far from a doctor, and to starve ragged in the winter! Why, a couple of winters ago I spent two months lying in a village north of here within the shadow of death. How I pulled through, it was a miracle! But for Nan, I'd be a gonner. I tell you, it's well enough to be a Traveller at this time of year, when you see the sun through the stinking mists, but when the frosts come – ah, the winter's a cruel time. Every summer, I spoil the bright days thinking of the cold ones what's in store."

"When it's spring again, you forget," Jess said. "Somehow the birds always return, no matter how much the madmen try to kill 'em, flying back over here from Russia and Africa and Scandinavia. And all these beastly weed killers they put down, what make the toughest cabbage wilt, aren't able to choke off the primrose and the nettle and the buttercup. We're real men then, the Travellers, when we hear our first cuckoo, aren't we, lads?"

This woman, Nan, attracted me. She was younger than the man she slept with, cleaner than most of them, and with wonderful wide blue eyes. I used to make a point of lying on the ground near her, so that I could watch her. I used to feast my eyes as if they were starving on the sweep of her legs, their almost straight line to the front, the cunning and varied curve of her calf. Sometimes I glimpsed also the fine width of her thighs. She took care of her legs, and she saw me looking at them. She and Jess made me want to become a Traveller ; but I still dreamed of escape, for freedom meant very little to me – their kind of freedom, I mean.

Nan talked to me. On the night we handed over the men who were trying for Africa, we met with another group of Travellers in underground warrens that had been carved out of an old mine. There we felt safe, and celebrated. I took Nan to one side, into a shallow gallery where we were alone and the lights of their lanterns hardly reached us. It smelt of earth cleaner than any we smelt above ground.

There, I slid my hands over those legs I so admired, I felt her generous body, and thrust my tongue between her lips. She allowed it for a while, let me do what I would, helped, and then drew back.

"You can't, Knowle, you know you can't! You're not a Traveller!"

We argued. At last she explained what she meant. There was a ritual of acceptance in becoming a Traveller. When you were trusted, you were sterilized and then were a fully fledged member of the band. Then you might have a woman, but not otherwise. In their hazardous way of life, babies were too much of a handicap to the Travellers. A pregnancy was as good as a

48

death sentence to a travelling woman.

It was the sourest example I ever knew of the fact that everything entails sacrifice.

The shock of this disclosure sent me that day into a hallucination. When I woke, Garry and Jess were kneeling by me, swabbing my face. A bandage was tied round my mouth; I had been screaming so loudly that even down the mine they became alarmed.

Weakly, I got up and accepted soup. They were on the move again, and we were to go back the way we had come. It was that time in autumn when the leaves are falling but the trees still have a cover to them. The nights through which we travelled were crisp and chill, and always I knew that I could never be a Traveller.

There came the night when again we slept together in the ruinous garage. On the next night's march, I recognized the landscape. Though it differed very little from the lands we had covered, I knew it because I had worked over it many a time. We were back near my village! Hammer snored not a mile away, snug in Dormitory Five.

Suppose I broke away – but they would punish me unless I could offer them something of value to them ... and at once I knew what that something could be.

Directly my thoughts had fallen into this way, I was like a man possessed. Either I must act now or not at all. My idiot plan was good for this very strip of earth I plodded over.

Uttering a brief cry, I fell face down into the soil.

"Get up, club foot," Garry said, pausing. I groaned. He bent over me. The two men behind came up and stopped. I went on groaning, developing it, building up the sound, though it made my hair stand on end inside my suit.

Though I could, of course, see nothing, I could hear that the Travellers were beginning to gather round me. "Spread out, you fools!" a woman said.

Someone gathered me up roughly and half-rolled me over so that they could peer at my face through the face-plate. I groaned the louder, changing it slowly to a sort of wailing noise that was more easy to keep up.

"He's having another of his bloody fits. Better leave him," someone said. This met with grunts of approval.

"He's no Traveller – he'll be dead by morning," another voice I recognized as Haagman's declared. "Leave them a bit of real fertilizer for their farm!"

They dropped me back on to the ground. Then I heard Jess's voice.

"We made the boy join us. He's one of us – what's how long he's been with us to do with the question? Are we rats to leave him lying in this furrow?"

"Don't give us that old nonsense, Jess," Haagman said harshly. "You know we're rats. And you know he's not a Traveller yet. Let's get on."

But Nan's voice came to me out of the darkness. "Knowle's in pain, Haagman."

"Huh, who isn't? The kid's dying! Listen at him!"

"All the more reason not to leave him!" Garry said.

Jess's voice came again, sharp and decisive. "Haagman, and you, Garry, get Knowle up between you and let's get moving. Carry him carefully."

When the decision was made, they did not argue. I felt their hands fumble for purchase along my rough suit – and then the lights came on!

Instantly, I knew that we were discovered. Perhaps my noise had given away our position. Though my blood froze, I was foolish enough not to know whether to be sorry or pleased. But at once something else happened that broke my nerve entirely. The brave and rugged men who called themselves Travellers fell down and screamed in terror. My horror and surprise were so great that I sat up and opened my eyes. I too uttered a strangled cry of fear.

We were surrounded by a row of devils.

Six of them stood there. They were metal-clad and shone in the lights carried by their companions. Two horns grew from their heads, their eyes gleamed with a cloudy redness that suggested hell fire.

In a minute I recognized them. They were the whole of our night patrol, from the village, and the Travellers were unlucky enough to cross their path. They were only machines, machines of a new model introduced only a month before I left. The Travellers had obviously never met with them before; certainly their shock value was great, materializing as they had done out of the night. Behind them stood two human figures, the Guard Commander and his Deputy. They strode forward with weapons raised.

"You are all under arrest. Any false move and we shoot to kill."

As if to emphasize their words, one of the Travellers sprang to his feet and dashed between two of the devil robots. Both machines blazed fire. The man fell flaming on to his face. We heard him crackle long after he had hit the ground.

We were made to get to our feet. Covered by the robots, the guards searched us and removed all weapons, unzipping our landsuits to do so. By this time, a whirler was hovering overhead, holding us all in a pool of radiance projected from a light in its belly. It was so bright that the worlds outside the light faded to nothing.

Then we had to march.

We did not go to the village, as I had expected. They took us the other way. We marched unbrokenly for four hours – no, not quite unbrokenly, for at one point two of the men tried to escape, one dashing in one direction, one in the other. The devils roasted them instantly.

At last we came to a long low building I had never seen before. It stood isolated among the crops. It was windowless and had only one low door. Directly I saw it, my heart began to hammer. The very look of the building told me it was there for no fair reason. Every line proclaimed that it existed for a bad purpose.

CHAPTER FIVE

THE irrational terror that sprang on me as we approached the sinister building must have snapped me into another of my unfortunate hallucinations. If so, I am unable to remember the details of it; that was the worst. When I remembered hallucinations, sometimes so clearly that they thenceforth became almost part of my life, it could be painful enough; but when I forgot them, and could recall no detail of them, they seemed to lie undigested in my mind, cold and dreadful.

Not that the sight I saw when I returned to my normal sense was not dreadful enough.

Twenty-three of us stood in the interior of the large shed,

guarded by the devils and the two guards, and illuminated by powerful lights that shone at us from a barrage of spotlights placed at chest level at one end of the chamber. It was not only the strange positioning of these lamps that contributed to our unease. Oh no! Behind us, the wall was pocked and chipped with bullet marks, most of them at about the height of a man's lung.

We stood motionless. No word was spoken. How long I had stood in my horrible trance, I have no means of knowing. The two guards did not wait as patiently as the devils, and walked now and then to the door. Evidently they were waiting for someone. But we were not allowed to move. If we needed to relieve ourselves, it had to be as we stood. I looked at Nan, but her pale face did not turn in my direction.

Finally someone arrived. We heard the noise of a hovercar landing outside. An officer in black uniform walked in and surveyed us.

He was a big man. His face was heavy, and he wore a heavy pair of spectacles. He looked at us without expression. His uniform was trim, and I guessed from his general appearance and from the delay he had caused that he had flown here from the city.

The guards now showed him some badges. These I recognized as prisoner's badges of the sort issued to everyone when they became landsmen. No doubt my own was there, taken from me during my fit of unconsciousness. This officer could read, for he checked the badges off against a thick list that he produced. At last he turned to us and addressed us.

His manner was curt, and what he had to say was brief.

"You are all landsmen and all of you have escaped. The penalty for escape you all know; it is death. By virtue of the authority invested in me by the central government, I have the power to impose this sentence upon you without further hindrance. Accordingly, I declare that you shall be executed by shooting where you stand."

As we drank in this edifying news, one of the guards who had marched us into the execution shed conferred with the officer; he nodded his head and looked serious. The Travellers peered frantically about for a way of escape, but the devil robots gave them absolutely no hope. Brave and hardened men that they were, they showed few signs of the terrible sense of impending dissolution that I felt; one of the women even smiled cynically and spat on the floor when the sentence was pronounced.

Again the officer came forward.

"I am told," he said, "that among you is the notorious gipsy known as Jess, for whose capture a reward is offered. Which of you is Jess? Step forward at once."

Nobody moved. I started to turn my head towards where I knew Jess stood, but at once someone dug me sharply in the back, and I stayed petrified. Silence.

"Come forward, you cowardly dog! We're going to make an example of you!"

Still no one moved. I felt my legs tremble.

"Very well," the officer barked. "The sentence of execution is stayed. Instead, you will all be taken to the Under-city for questioning. Perhaps some of you know what that means."

The Under-city, I should explain, is the considerable area, mainly used for urban services such as the disposal of sewage and rubbish, under the great platform on which a city perches. The police notoriously have their interrogation headquarters there, and there are legends about their methods of questioning.

"You have one last chance. Jess must step out at once."

The threat was effective. Someone moved forward. So did someone else, and another, and another. Every Traveller there took a pace forward, women as well as men. I was carried forward with them.

The officer went red in the face but controlled himself. He pointed a finger at the Traveller nearest to him. "What is your name?"

"I am Jess." In fact it was a man I knew to be called Burgess.

The officer asked a second and a third. All gave the same reply: "I am Jess." All were protecting the leader from what they knew would be protracted torture and death.

Now the officer was icy calm.

"Very well," he said. "I shall order the robots to fire at your legs. You will all lie here and die slowly. The only man who shall be spared is the man who comes forward and points out this leader Jess to me."

Ah, the shame of it! How many times since then have I asked myself why a man's whole life should be judged by one minute of it. And then again I ask myself why it should not be so judged. And why should it not be so judged indeed, when I am the judge and can select the criteria?

I ran forward to the officer, crying to him that I would tell, crying that I had no part of the others, that I was not a Traveller, that – it doesn't matter what I cried.

They were clever, the Travellers! Though they had been searched, two of them had managed to hide throwing-knives in their clothes. They threw them at me.

That grim and solid officer had not known when he called for a traitor that he called his own death. For the knives missed me. I was weak in the legs and ankles with fear, and I half-fell as I ran forward. So I heard the knives go by. Both caught the officer in the chest.

He jerked his hands up, slapping his own face in a wild gesture that sent his spectacles flying. His heavy face crumpled and he fell forward. Almost before he had hit the floor, the quicker of the guards had barked an order to the devil robots. They opened fire immediately on the Travellers. Oh, Nan! Oh, Jess!

When it was all over, and the last echo had been wrung from under the grim roof, I was marched into the darkness outside. A hovercar waited there with another officer beside it. I remember seeing his face and thinking that he looked more scared than I. My hands were clipped together and I was bundled into the hovercar.

I cannot recount in detail the madness of the succeeding weeks. I have always thought of them as weeks, though they may in fact have been days or months. In the heart of the Under-city, to which I was taken, it was hard, even under the best conditions, to tell the difference between day and night. I underwent three prolonged interrogations, and was otherwise left alone in a solitary cell. The cell was without windows, although it had a lavatory and a bunk and was heated – just as well, since I was stripped naked and allowed no stitch of clothing. No means that I know of is so effective in reducing a man's morale and nerves to pulp. Yet I must have been lucky ; I was not tortured.

They did not torture me. In the circumstances, I was able

to do that easily enough for myself, wondering how I had acted the betrayer so casually.... There was a pile of pages here I wrote about mind, but we had better keep to body.

One day, a guard came for me. He threw me a pair of trousers and prodded me immediately out of the cell, so that I had to put the garment on as best I could as I went along. Instead of going to the interrogation room as I had done before, I was marched out of the building and handed over to another guard, who eyed for me – that is, gave up a print of his retinal pattern as was sometimes done in the cities; in an earlier age, he would have signed for me, I suppose.

He bundled me into the front of a small scooter-thing, which moved off at once. I remember looking up and seeing overhead, instead of sky, a great black and brown shield on which moisture gleamed. At first I mistook it for a lowering storm cloud. My mind was sluggish from misery; it took some while before I realized that this was a view of the city respectable citizens never saw: its mighty metal underbelly. In my low state, the sight completely demoralized me; I was crushed by it.

I was taken before the Farmer.

At the time, I thought that this was the most terrible thing that could happen to me. The Farmer was a legend; he was the begetter of all our troubles; he was Evil Incarnate ... and I found myself shivering in a small bare office confronting him.

"Sit down on that chair and stop shaking," he said.

What had I imagined he would look like? Had I imagined fangs, a mountainous body? He was small and neat and tense. Although his hair was white, he wore a small black beard, and his eyebrows were also black. His nose was sharp and aquiline and his mouth firm. These features instantly became the characteristics of death in my mind.

He observed me steadily and then pressed a buzzer under his hand. A woman appeared; he asked her to fetch a blanket. Until she returned, he sat silent, observing me without saying a word. I hung my head and could not meet his gaze. When the blanket came, he stood up and tossed it to me.

"Put that round you," he said.

When I had done what he told me, he began to speak.

At first he asked about the Travellers, as my interrogators

had done earlier. Then he asked about life in the village. Slowly, I began to talk more freely. It even came out that I could read and found books in the ruined town.

"So occasionally you went to that ruin, where you had a secret meeting with – books," he said.

"I did not go there often, sir. That was why I missed seeing the Travellers before, sir, when they passed that way."

"But you went there as often as you dared, Noland."

"Yes, sir."

"You'll never have come across a book called '1984', I suppose?"

"No, sir."

"There's a young man in that book who is regarded as an enemy by his rulers. He also goes to a secret meeting-place. There he meets another human – a woman with whom he is in love. But you met only books. Weren't you ever lonely?"

I did not know what he was talking about. I could not answer. He changed his tack then, saying sharply: "You're just a fool, Noland, nothing more harmful than that. You should never have become mixed up with the Travellers. Also, I have a report from a doctor who says you suffer from a form of hallucination. Is that so?"

Since I could not tell whether he wanted me to say yes or no, I replied that I supposed so.

"Yes, or no, you fool? Do you or don't you have hallucinations?"

"Yes, sir, thank you." My brain was numb.

"I'm going to let you go free, Noland. If I don't do so, you'll spend the rest of a short life festering somewhere down under the city because nobody will know what to do with you. Do you understand?"

"Yes, sir."

"I don't suppose you do. In this case, I can intervene because you are on record as being the man who betrayed or almost betrayed Gipsy Jess. You did, didn't you?"

"I didn't mean it, sir. I –"

"Silence immediately! As his betrayer, you are entitled to a considerable reward. I am going to see that you get it, and with it will ensure that you buy a job I shall provide. Do you have a family?"

"Yes – no, sir."

56

"Have you no parents?"

"I come from an orphanage."

"Have you any idea what sort of a job you would be good at?"

"No, sir."

"For God's sake, man, I know you've been ill-treated, but try and get a grasp of your faculties now that someone's trying to help."

"I didn't mean to betray Jess, sir, really."

"The less often you say that the better. In fact, you'd be better out of the country. Ever been to sea?"

"I'm afraid not, sir."

"You'll soon get used to it."

"Yes, sir."

He summoned the woman again. It was then that I heard the name *Trieste Star* for the first time. After that, I was taken back to the Under-city. I rotted there for more uncounted days before I was dragged into daylight again, given clothes, and sent to join the freighter in a northern port.

I never saw the Farmer again. But I kept the blanket with me that he gave me during the interview; it was still with me when, twelve years later, I ran his ship aground on the Skeleton Coast.

CHAPTER SIX

STARS shone in a paling sky. Soon they would all dissolve as the light increased. I lay on the bridge of the *Trieste Star*, staring up at the sky. I had been dissolved myself.

Slowly I rolled over and stood up. The freighter was sailing on, though with a heavy list to starboard, ploughing in through the heart of Africa, following the Tropic of Capricorn across the land, our keel cutting through bedrock, our screws churning deep through a sullen sea of clay. My head cleared, and I saw the situation as it really was, the wrecked ship lying in shallow water, the beach ahead – the beach that, merging into desert, was still beach a hundred miles inland.

The instruments on the bridge still functioned, or some of them did. It was the sound of them, more than anything, that had given me the illusion that we were still at sea. I thought of the decks below me. The automatic things would be down there, crawling about their business as if nothing had happened! I looked instinctively at the gauges on the nuclear power board. Several needles were well over into the red. The delicate servometers that controlled the reactor had been put out of action when we struck; unattended, they would reach critical mass and blow the ship all over Africa.

But that was not my worry. It would take me only a few moments to rejoin Doctor Thunderpeck and the spastic, Abdul Demone. What worried me was how I had got on to the bridge, for the last thing I remembered was settling down exhaustedly by Thunderpeck's fire. No doubt my hallucinations had entered a new phase, and when I dreamed of the Travellers I had been impelled to travel, and had come back to the ship. But why had I thought the ship was moving?

Then I heard it and knew I heard it. Somewhere, an engine throbbed, and not the freighter's. I peered forward. A mist lay over the beach, the sort of mist that brings chill to a tropic morning, a mist that forecasts heat and is sucked away with the sun.

In all the still-unlit universe, only there on that stony beach did I have friends. I could see them, Thunderpeck and Abdul. Beside them was a tracked vehicle, the throbbing I had heard coming from its engine. No doubt it had been that sound which woke me. The vehicle was a light tank, flying the flag of New Angola. Six armed men had climbed out of it. In their midst stood my two friends. Their hands were raised above their heads.

Even as I looked, one of the Angolans stepped forward and began to search them. I saw Abdul back away. The searcher struck him across the side of the neck. Hampered by the iron on his leg, Abdul stumbled on to his knees in the sand, and was roughly hauled up again.

I waited to see no more.

This must have been an isolated New Angola patrol. No one else would be about in such a desolate place. Our position lay on the fringe of Angolese territory and near the newly-founded Waterberg State, if I had my bearings right. The patrol looked as if it was in a hurry – which meant that it would be ruthless. And it had something to be ruthless about:

the freighter. The *Trieste Star* was a valuable piece of salvage. I found myself regretting that I had beached her.

I guéssed what the patrol's next move would be. They would send a boarding party out to look over the ship.

Although the *Trieste Star* was only a freighter, there was a small armoury in the captain's cabin. I ran down on to "A" deck. One of the deck swabbers was at work, mopping away with a crabwise motion against the list. I hated the thing.

My cabin was as it had been. A twinge of nostalgia touched me. I had been the lowest member of the crew when I first came aboard but, because of illness and a case of madness, it had taken me only four years to become captain ; since the rank carried almost no responsibilities with it, it was little but a name. For all that, this cabin had been home, and the best I had ever known, for the last eight years. My hand went absently to my breast pocket. The love letters from Justine to another man were still there ; they, too, were the best I had ever known.

Using my key, I unlocked the armoury door. It was little more than a locker. Inside were a couple of sasers for use against ship's robots that might go wrong and prove dangerous, and a tracer-firing gun obviously for use against men. I checked the gun over and collected a can of ammunition. I hurried back with my load to the bridge and set the gun up ready to fire.

I had never worked a gun of this type, although I knew how to do so. What I knew I could never do was aim so that I hit the Angolese and missed Thunderpeck. I set up the gun and then sat there fuming, watching the indignity of my friends ashore.

The tableau changed. Thunderpeck and Abdul were ushered back towards the tracked vehicle by two of the soldiers, while the others came forward. This I could not see clearly, for at that moment the sun rose almost clear of the low mist and shone straight into my eyes.

Even as I cursed the sun and the planet on which it shone, an idea came to me. Shading my eyes, I made out the party of four soldiers at the water's edge, about to launch the raft on which we had paddled ashore the previous night. As I had surmised, they were about to board the freighter. They would think only of coming to the starboard side, where a rope ladder dangled, inviting them up. Lugging the gun again, I made haste to port.

For my idea was simple. They presented no target now, and would be out of sight in a moment, concealed by the bulk of the ship. Once I gave my presence away, they would be after me. To preserve the element of surprise, I must get ashore and lie in wait for them – preferably behind their vehicle. From that point, I would be able to ambush them perfectly when they returned.

Lashing a rope round the port rail, I tied the machine-gun to the other end, lowered it until it slithered down the steep slope of the side and dangled over the water, and then secured it there. Wrenching open one of the deck lockers – I worked in a sweat, I can tell you! – I pulled out another of the self-inflating rafts. Before it was properly distended, I flung myself down into the sea. It opened up on the surface like a grotesque water-lily. Running down the steep side, I plunged in after it, to come up panting close by.

I heaved myself on to the raft, paddled across to where the gun dangled, unslipped the knot that secured it and laid it on the raft; then I was paddling for shore. The bulk of the *Trieste Star* hid me from the boarding party.

Once I was ashore and moving up the slope of sand, danger threatened most from the vehicle ahead; but I counted on the Angolese inside being too busy keeping Thunderpeck and Abdul quiet to worry about the outside world for a moment.

Certain men are naturally men of action. Perhaps to them my movements would have seemed a matter of course; to me, even at the time, they were a matter of wonder. I was not born a man of action; and yet, and yet – oh, there was an exhilaration, beyond the mere goad of the fear of death, in pelting across that white beach with the gun cradled in my arms! The bullets that spattered at my heels were an added savoury.

Only as I flung myself under the vehicle, sprawling down between the two cogged tracks, did I realize that the fire came not from the vehicle itself but from the ship. My timing had not been as good, my haste not as speedy, as I had imagined. The four Angolese had climbed already on to the deck of the freighter and were sniping at me.

This, of course, came into my head in an instant. I knew it without looking round. Just as well I did not! Goaded on with fear, I grovelled behind the light tank, burrowing my way into the sand.

The shots attracted the alarm of the soldiers in the vehicle. The hatch slammed up, I heard an exclamation above me. At any moment, the Angolese would look down and see me.

In that fearful moment, I knew I was not a man of action – my nerve gave. I could not rise to meet him, to challenge my fate. I could only burrow spinelessly into the sand, awaiting the fatal shot.

It was then that the universe erupted.

First it was light, then sound, then a terrible heat that shrivelled my skin. I died then, or if I didn't, I knew death. Consciousness was consumed in a great crimson inferno. When I crawled, minutes later, stunned and stifled, out of my self-dug pit, the tracked vehicle was burning ; over the sea, rising high into the morning air, was an ugly pall of smoke, familiar in shape, the remains of a mighty fire ball. Of the *Trieste Star,* little was left but scattered wreckage up and down the beach. Of the New Angolese patrol, there was no sign.

The freighter's nuclear heart had burst! Though by a freak it had saved me, I was now alone without provisions on the dreaded coast. I sank back into my pit of sand, trying to think, trying not to fear.

I lay in the pit of sand until the intolerable heat of the burning vehicle drove me out. By then, I thought, much of the radiation should have passed. The cloud of smoke that hung over the shore was drifting far out to sea on the breeze, and this I took as a good sign that danger was being carried away from me. But I was terribly ignorant of radiation hazard, and could only hope that, sheltered as I had been, I had escaped a lethal dose.

Now it seemed advisable to get away from this grim spot as soon as possible.

Accordingly, I rose and started along the beach at a steady jog-trot. I headed south, for it was in that direction that I had seen from the bridge of the *Trieste Star* a tower a little way down the coast.

Although the power of the sun was already strong, I had high hopes of finding the city and saving myself from death in the desert. In my mind I made an inventory of the things I had. But what had I but the clothes that now began to cling damply to me and, in my inner pocket, the bundle of those tantalizing letters from a woman called Justine to a man called Peter? Certainly I had no water or food. The inventory was so brief and depressing that I closed it, and concentrated on moving rapidly down the beach. It was another time for body above mind.

I paused when I saw a GEM speeding along the foreshore in my direction. The dramatic end of the *Trieste Star* must have been heard and registered fifty miles away, and would surely have attracted attention. I feared that this oncoming vehicle might contain a detachment of troops from New Angola ; but even if they came from Waterberg State, which lay south of here, I knew they might very well be hostile. Although Africa was uneasily at peace with itself after a succession of civil wars, it was only the very strong President, Abdul el Mahasset, who kept the nations under him from warring again, as many of them had made war on South Africa some decades ago. It might be difficult for me to establish my peaceful intent after the firework display I had just provided on their doorstep.

So I stood on the beach, shading my eyes and watching the craft come near. It was a sledge-shaped hovercraft with a canvas hood which had been folded back, so that I could see the heads of the men inside. Everything was pearly clear in the sunlight.

The craft executed a showy half-circle, flinging up sand, and drew to a halt facing back the way it had come, sinking on to the beach as it did so. A tall black man in a colourful silk skull cap and long robes climbed out and walked over to me as I stood there uncertainly. I was relieved to see that neither he nor his companion, the driver, were in military uniform, though it gave me no great pleasure to see the automatic weapon he held in his hand. He kept it levelled at me as he came forward.

"Whoever you are, come with us," he said.

"Wait a minute – who are you? Where are you going?"

He motioned with the gun.

"No time for talk or argument. We are going to Walvis Bay ; you come with us quickly, before there is trouble."

"What sort of trouble are you expecting?"

He shook his great grey head as if in reproach. "You want

Angolese to get a hold of you, man? Do as I say and hurry up!"

On the whole, this did not sound as if they directed a deal of antagonism at me. I was, in any case, not in very good shape to argue. As I climbed up the steel ladder into the GEM, I glanced back down the beach to where the freighter had been. A figure was coming towards us, lifting a hand and waving as it came.

Hot though I was, chill came over me. That black face, surely I recognized it, surely it was the Figure? Even here on this parched strand, it seemed I could not shake off that phantom who pursued me. Then I saw it was Doctor Thunderpeck, and sighed with relief.

At the same time, the driver of the GEM muttered an exclamation and pointed. He pointed not at Thunderpeck but inland. A light tank was racing towards us, flying the flag of New Angola. At once the tall man pushed me into the craft, the driver revved the engine, and we lifted.

"My friend! Don't leave my friend!" I shouted, grasping the tall man by the arm and pointing towards Thunderpeck.

The tall man, whose name I found later was Israt, spoke sharply to the driver. We wheeled again and scudded low over the beach towards Thunderpeck, showering grit as we went. I leant over the side of the cabin and extended an arm to him. Hovering, we stopped just long enough for him to swing himself up through the blast and noise of our air column; then we turned once more and headed in the direction from which the GEM had originally come.

The light tank showed every sign of hostile intent. It was ploughing forward at a great rate, heading for a point where its course would intersect ours. The strategy was obvious. If they could get underneath us and spill our air, we would crash. They were already doing their best to ensure this by directing a haser at us. Once, a burn slashed across our side, narrowly missing us; but with the combined speeds of the two vehicles and the bumpiness of the going, their aim with a thin-beamed heat weapon was not good.

They brought a loud-hailer into play.

"That vehicle! That vehicle! Halt before we destroy you! You are violating the El Mahasset Treaty! This is New Angola territory. Stop before we knock you out the air!"

We replied with another burst of speed. We were almost at the point where our tracks would intersect the other vehicle's. Since our craft seemed to be a civilian machine, we had no weapons with which to defend ourselves. At the last moment, the driver swerved out to the right, skidding low over a bar of shingle, and bounced out to sea in a great sweep of spray.

As we plunged on, I looked back. The tank, unable to kill its speed in time, ploughed across the bar of shingle and plunged into the ocean. I cheered and turned to see how pleased Thunderpeck was. But Thunderpeck had collapsed.

For the first time, I wondered how he had survived the nuclear detonation and in what sort of shape he was. I had assumed he was immolated inside the burning tracked vehicle.

Israt passed me a vacuum flask with iced water in. Some of this I forced down Thunderpeck's throat, afterwards taking a hearty swig myself. He revived then, partially at least, and explained what had happened inside the vehicle during those fateful moments when the freighter's pile blew. When one of the Angolese soldiers climbed up to see what the shouting was about, the other tried to tie up the doctor and Abdul Demone. Thunderpeck offered him some resistance, and the soldier knocked him down on to the floor. That action had been his saving. He had fallen under a table when the interior of the tank was suddenly filled with flame. He had covered his head to protect it from kicks but still saw the fire, even through closed eyes. He guessed at once what had happened, since only one thing could have caused such a wave of heat.

Shocked, he staggered up. Abdul and the soldier were still on their feet but already burning fiercely. The shock must have killed them stone-dead ; of the other Angolese, there was no sign. The blast must have carried him out and spread him across miles of desert.

Half-stifled by the heat, and with his lungs afire, Thunderpeck managed to climb out of the turret and fling himself down on to the sand on the other side of the vehicle from me. Though the sand was burning, he managed to scoop himself a hole where he could lie covered until the particles with shorter half-lives had dispersed.

Before he had finished telling me this, we were approaching the town I came to know as Walvis Bay.

I will leave a description of this city until later. It is sufficient to record here that it was not built upon a platform, as were all the other cities of which I had ever heard, but stood direct on a stony promontory overlooking the sea. This was by no means its sole peculiarity, but when we first looked at it, we noticed only that it possessed a number of spires pointing to the sky, so that it presented a spiked outline against the desert ; our cities have no spires and few high buildings.

The way to the city was barred by a slow-flowing yellow stream, the Swakop, which presented no obstacle to our GEM. On the far bank were set up barbed wire and sentry boxes and gun emplacements, and all the traditional equipment of a frontier ; but when a signalman there waved a signal flag at us, we swerved to follow the river and entered Walvis Bay from the sea-front.

We had no time to admire the fantastic architectural effects, for it was now made apparent to us that although we had been rescued, we had also been captured. Thunderpeck and I had our wrists clipped together and were made to dismount from the GEM, which sank to a stop. We were marched across a wide promenade and into a towering white building.

"Where are we being taken?" I asked the tall black man.

"I shall get orders from my superiors, and they will decide what will happen to you. It is useless to ask me questions."

"Who are your superiors?"

"I told you, it is useless to ask questions."

The building we had entered was no prison. It suggested rather a luxury hotel, though the luxury was as yet of a rather rudimentary kind. The foyer was equipped in extremely sumptuous taste, panelled with exotic woods, ceilinged with a three-dimensional representation of night sky, ornamented with magnificent plants and trees, many of them apparently growing from the floor. Yet the floor itself was of naked concrete, and that chiselled away in some parts to reveal cables running underneath. Carpenters' trestles obstructed our way, insulation panels were piled against a wall mosaic. The stairs were sumptuously carpeted, although the decorators ladders lying there against the balustrade ruined the effect aimed for.

Some men, three of them, sat smoking and leaning against ornamental pillars as we went by ; they paid no attention to us. We were led up to the first floor, and there separated. Thunderpect was thrust through one door, I through another. The man who had picked us up in the desert came into my room with me.

He ran his hands – with obvious distaste – through my clothes, taking out anything he found in my pockets and throwing it into a bag he placed on a side table. Helplessly, I watched those strange letters from the unknown Justine being thrown into the bag.

When the fellow had skinned me of everything, he nodded solemnly to me.

"Behave yourself here for a little while ; I shall be back." And with that he took up the bag and left me. I heard the door lock behind him.

I was in a sort of washroom which had another door to it. Before I tried to investigate that – I was sure I would find it locked – I staggered over to the wash-basin and turned on the cold tap, for I was faint from the ordeal of the day. A trickle of rust ran from the tap, then nothing. I tried the other tap, the hot one ; nothing came. Dust lay in the basin.

Suddenly overcome by nausea, I sat back on the little table and closed my eyes. At once the world seemed to recede from me at a great rate. In alarm, I tried to open my eyes again. The lids had taken on an immense weight. Through the lashes, as a man through bars sees his executioner, I saw the Figure approaching. I could do nothing.

He came from a long way off, his damned eye on me. That black countenance – why should it have the power to paralyse my soul? The Figure came to me, stood against me, and released me from the metal clip that held my wrists together. Then again the world receded, for how long I could not tell. When I roused once more, a beautiful and fatal woman was regarding me.

CHAPTER SEVEN

IMMENSITY. That is part of my illusion; I struggle to express it in words. Even for the short while I jog-trotted between desert and sea, running for the promised shelter of a city, I was aware of the being of the desert and the sea. I knew that on a planetary scale those two great creations were heaving with an activity meaningless to man.

From that Figure I drew something like the same impression of an immense process, relevant to me yet unfathomable. If that Figure was a product of my mind, how uncomfortable to know that in my mind too the unknowable things ground on.

An echo of that unease came to me as the strange woman confronted me – or I thought it was an echo, though I may have been as misled as those who think they hear the sea in a seashell, when they listen only to the whisper of their own bloodstream. But certainly my first thought before her fine pallor was that I had the privilege of another glimpse at the workings of that inscrutable machine.

So it was fitting that her opening remark should lack all meaning to me: "So you are the sort of desperado von Vanderhoot uses!"

My intelligence was still silted up with sand.

"Who are you?" I asked.

"Has Israt not told you? Or do you not know?"

"I have learnt nothing here, except that there are thieves and bullies in Walvis Bay."

She raised an eyebrow. "I would say from what Israt tells me that you know a great amount more than that. You must surely be intelligent enough to understand that a pretence of ignorance will not save you."

"Save me from what? I pretend nothing. I know nothing of what happens in Walvis Bay. Until today, it was just a name on the map to me."

She sighed and made a dismissive gesture with one slender hand.

"I suppose you pretend you have no connection with von Vanderhoot."

The name meant nothing to me; I was utterly at a loss and said so.

With a trace of cruel amusement on her lips, she said: "You really are in for trouble."

She regarded me with detachment; I looked at her with considerably more involvement. For one thing, if I were in for trouble – of the nature of which I had no inkling at that time – then this woman was clearly capable of helping me.

For another, she was of a compelling type of beauty.

The usual look of illness that marked most of the world's undernourished population was stamped upon her. But in her it seemed inborn, almost as much a spiritual characteristic as a physical one; she had transformed it into an aspect of mystery and mental hunger. Her form, though well shaped, was slight, and she reinforced its emaciation by wearing a black gown that swept down to her ankles except at the front, where it lifted up to her thighs, revealing a rich lining of scarlet.

Her hair framed a thin and pale face, the perfection of her features – almost translucent, they seemed to me – being set off against her dark and rather lank hair. In the hair was one thick lock of white that curled away from her forehead; yet she appeared youthful; yet she appeared to be of no definite age. Her manner was languid, but I detected an underlying tension. Though she was fragile, there was determination in her. She woke in me a tender and hopeless desire; while at the same time I recognized that I feared her.

"Who are you?" I asked her again.

Again came that contemptuous smile.

"I think you know very well that I am Justine Smith."

"Justine! My Justine!" I gasped the words as if they wounded my lips; I think she hardly understood what I said. Inclining her head to my confusion, she said: "Before I take you to Peter, you had better come into my suite and wash yourself. I will get you some clothes to replace your rags. Peter is fastidious."

Peter ... the man to whom she had written the letters.... And I saw at once that these rather tortured documents might well have come from this elegant and subtle creature.

"Who is Peter?" I asked her.

She was not answering. She was turning, she was clapping her hands. At once a small black boy ran forward and bowed to her as she moved into the other room. She stood in the middle of this room and raised one arm to point to another door.

"Go through there and get yourself washed. There is water in the bath. The boy will bring you a robe in a minute."

The room in which she stood was imposingly luxurious. Her fine profile was framed by a window from which a balcony commanded a view of the unresting Atlantic. Without will,

I went where she pointed, and entered into her bathroom.

Inevitably an erotic curiosity stirred in me. I took in the thick hangings that masked the window, and the great blue tub, almost a small swimming-pool, that stood half-surrounded by mirrors, and a row of bottles that contained strange colours and scents. A large dolphin stood at one end of the little pool ; pressure on its tail brought the water gushing forth. Someone could afford to keep Justine in a luxurious suite. It seemed a pity that even here, in this exotic holy of holies, the water should be tinged orange with sand or rust.

I was glad enough to wash, but as I cleaned myself, wild and frightening thoughts ran through my head. What sort of arrangement I had stumbled into I did not know, nor could I determine how I felt about the beautiful woman who proved to be the writer of those love letters. As I scrubbed myself, I remembered that in fact the letters had contained little that might be called an ordinary love. Most of them had been about something else, something which I neither understood nor cared about: African politics. Now I cursed myself that I had not followed them more closely, for they might have provided a clue to what was happening.

While I was drying myself, the boy came in with a nylon robe. Although I had never worn anything like it before, and felt self-conscious in it, I put it on in preference to most of the stained and tattered rags I had taken off.

Acting on sudden curiosity, I went to the tall drapes and pulled them apart. There was the sea. There, to the left, was Justine's balcony. She had come out on to it and stood looking down, but really not looking at all, in an attitude that suggested extreme sorrow. In that moment, I decided I must win her support: it also came to me that I loved her.

As I went back into the other room, she came from the balcony to me.

"I saw from the bathroom window that you looked very sad out there."

"Not at all. I suffer from a fear of heights."

"Then why do you stand out there?"

"I always try to conquer my fears. Don't you?"

That silenced me for a minute, then I plunged in again. "Justine," I said, "you must believe that I have arrived here in all innocence, and entirely by accident. I know nothing of what goes on here, nor of this von Vanderhoot – was that his name? – of whom you speak. Please believe me."

She looked me up and down with her long eyelashes lying almost against her cheeks.

"You pleb!" she said, "you are so obviously mixed up in this intrigue, how can you hope to lie your way out of it?"

Angrily, I stepped forward and seized her wrists. Though she struggled, I clutched her tightly.

"I tell you I know nothing about anything. Who is this von Vanderhoot of whom you speak, and why should I know him?"

"He is a spy in the pay of the New Angolese, as you are. He is an old old man with a bad heart condition that makes it necessary for him to go about in one of these new gravity harness things. Israt was out in the desert searching for von Vanderhoot when he caught you."

A little light began to dawn. Von Vnaderhoot must have been the dead man whose body, still supported in its anti-gravity harness, had fetched up against the *Trieste Star* – the man from whom I had rescued Justine's letters!

"Von Vanderhoot is dead!" I exclaimed, releasing her.

"So you admit you know him, then –"

"No, I don't – I mean, I knew nothing about him, or who he was. If I was an enemy of yours, would I have run so willingly to your friend Israt to give myself up?"

That seemed to make her hesitate. I plunged on.

"Listen to me, Justine! This man was dead when I found him. He died and his anti-grav unit carried him out to sea. I took the letters out of his pocket and read them. I am able to read well. You wrote them, didn't you? Well, I loved those letters. They were strange and exciting. I have had too little love in my life. I fell in love with them. Now that I have you, their writer, here, I transfer that love to you. I would die for you, Justine."

"Ah, would you?" she said, that cruel smile moving her lips again. I expelled to the back of my mind, where it habitually lived, the thought that I had been unable to die for Jess or March Jordill. Fervently, I said: "Yes, Justine, I would die for you if circumstances demanded it. But you know that at present I am helpless. Help me first to get free, and then I will be your rejoicing slave for life."

She stood back and laughed. It was a small cold sound.

"I am now convinced of your innocence! If you were not innocent, you would not misread the situation so badly. How can I help you to get free? I am as much a prisoner as you are."

While I digested this news, Israt entered and bowed to Justine.

"Madam, I have spoken with Mr. Mercator about our new arrivals. He wishes to see them and you at his hotel. At once."

"Very well. Where is the other prisoner?"

"I have him outside."

She gestured to me. I followed as she walked proudly to the door. We went downstairs, through the foyer, and into the street, where the sunlight lay in breathless pools. An aroma of cooking drifted to me, and I realized how hungry I was.

Two large cars of an old-fashioned non-automatic kind were drawn up outside the hotel. I saw Thunderpeck was sitting in the rear one, and managed to wave to him before I was pushed into the first. I sat in the back with Justine, while Israt sat in the front with the driver.

"Who is this man Mercator we are going to see?" I asked.

"You do not imagine the proper way to court me is to ask for a boring stream of information, do you?"

"Justine, don't play with me. If my life is at stake, I must know whom I am going to be confronted by."

She made a *moue* of disgust, as if she found dramatics distasteful.

"Peter Mercator is the man to whom I wrote those letters you seem so over-heated about."

"I've never heard of him."

"That tells me more about you than about him. He is one of the most powerful men in the English State of United Europe."

"I know nothing about politics, nothing at all."

"Pooh, you seem to know nothing about anything. You'd better be a bit sharper in front of Mercator."

"Listen – I can read, Justine! I told you. Can an ignorant man read? Why do you hold so low an opinion of me?"

She turned and stared at me as if seeing me for the first time. Her haughty and lovely lips pouted. "You pleb!" she said. "I have a low opinion of all men."

In a fury, I said: "Listen, I'm not going to the slaughter like a lamb. I've no wish to meet Mercator unprepared like this. If you care for anything, if you have a heart, prepare me, so that I can fight for both of us, if fighting is needed."

But she made a dismissive gesture with her hand.

"Why should you not die? Why should I not die? Is the world not too full of beastly people already — twenty-two thousand million of them, or whatever the disgusting figure is? Do you think I care what Peter does with either of us?"

"I care if you don't! I've had to spend most of my life fighting to live — and I'll fight to make you live! Help me now, Justine, and I swear I'll help you, and give you something to live for."

"I've told you, I cannot help you."

"Yes, you can! I am going to open the car door and jump. Knock down Israt's gun when he fires at me, and let me escape down one of these side alleys."

"I warn you, I am a crack shot myself."

"You would not fire at me, Justine. Remember, I have read your heart, I know you are too gentle. Knock down his arm when I jump."

"Oh, stop these melodramatics and come sensibly to Peter."

"Where does this man live, where?"

"He is at the South Atlantic Hotel, and we shall —"

"See you there sometime, Justine, my sweet!"

I flung open the car door and jumped.

It was not too perilous. The driver was having to move slowly, picking his way through a bazaar; and the narrowness of the way was impeded by builder's lorries.

A dark shop with brass objects piled into its window stood to one side. Using my momentum, I dashed through its open doorway into the interior. And incendiary bullet followed me in, wanged sharply over my shoulder, buried itself in the far wall, and burst into flame. I had heard of this weapon, but never seen it in action. Its light was so bright, I was blinded. Gobbets of flaring lead spewed out of the wall at me. So Justine had not knocked Israt's arm aside!

In the shop was an old woman, bent double with disease. She gave a shriek and bolted for a rear door when I came rushing in. The brilliance had blinded me too much to see properly, but I was able to follow her. Behind was a narrow cluttered yard, bathed in vertical sunlight. There I could see enough to dive over the wall at the far end.

I landed almost on top of a gaunt Arab, knocked him sprawling as I sprawled, picked myself up, and doubled fast between two windowless houses still in the last stages of building. I passed a man in a fez. As he stood back, I snatched the hat from his head and rammed it on to my own; any sort of partial disguise might help against my enemies.

Rounding two more corners, I had to drop panting into a slower pace. No sounds of pursuit came from behind, but I did not allow that to reassure me.

I was in a strange area, a nondescript dumping-ground, covered with all sorts of scaffolds and building materials, paint, mortar, wood, plastic, brick, and clay. The area was bounded by what I took for a moment to be a sort of variegated wall; then I realized what it was: it was a line of false buildings and shops, and I was sandwiched between the two lines of their façades. An unease filled me – I mean an unease over and above the natural high state of apprehension into which the chase had thrown me.

Once again I was made conscious of the thinness of reality. Life, in that moment, seemed to me something wafer thin, like a gaudy poster one might tear from a wall to reveal the true solid substance beneath. I paused, swaying, so that I had to put my hands out to prevent myself falling.

A sweet and strange smell assailed my nostrils – was it violets or wallflowers, or was it onions cooking? I say strange, and strange it seemed, yet I knew I had smelt it before, without being able to recall where. Almost, I fell, but someone touched my fingertips. I turned and it was Justine.

"This way, Knowle, let me show you," she said.

"I thought –"

"There's no time to waste!"

She ran forward. She opened one of the false doors, and we ran through into a false corridor. It looked like a corridor, but had no ceiling, and was open to the sky. Because it sloped at a strange angle, I could see the ocean. Underfoot was the beach. We ran down it to another building. At first I thought it was a cathedral, but it proved to be a sort of hotel. Inside, it was filled with unshaped chunks of plastics. Justine

73

seemed tireless, running up flight after flight of stairs. At last she stopped before a door, and I caught up with her, gasping until I feared my lungs might burst out of my mouth.

"Go in," she said, opening the door.

It was a sort of living-room, and crowded with plants and ornamental trees, some of which grew out of the floor.

There were also machines, thin and spiky like old sculpture, with tiny vanes that rotated and bubbled, that moved behind perspex; these machines grew as certainly as did the plants. I was frightened, for the foliage obscured the farther wall, and I felt exposed to danger. When I turned to look at Justine, I saw how thin and pale she was; instinctively I move to her to take her into my arms. The Figure was there before me! He must have been hiding behind one of the trees, giving his ancient black gaunt look.

Angrily, I seized him by the collar. I was aware of his blazing my breath on my cheek, then he was gone again.

"Who was that?" I demanded of Justine, secretly testing to see if she had noticed him.

"He only comes to see you when you are near death," she told me.

"Then why should he touch you?"

Again that cruel smile that I knew by heart.

"I am always near to death. I hate all human life, and death is my ally."

There was a couch among the trees, with a dim light burning over it. I suggested to her that she lie down and rest on it. She agreed, but said that first she must water her plants. She took up a can with a long spout, bright red in colour; she walked among the trees and machines with this, watering them at their roots. I lay down on another couch and watched her.

When Justine had finished her task, she returned to her bed, placing the red can beside it. She lay down. I wished to go to her, but found myself unable to. It was as if the can prevented me; she had the can, I had not.

Now I saw that something was happening to the trees. They were writhing in a disturbing fashion. I was frightened until I realized that they were dying, shivering as they did so in a vegetable death agony. In the air was the odour of Oxbenzide; I remembered it clearly from my years on the land. Justine had poisoned the plants, though whether by accident or intent

I did not know. The leaves were turning brown, branches and stalks drooping and growing sickly.

In despair, I went over to Justine. I could hardly see her. She looked very small and white and insignificant. I called her name, but she never moved. Her lips were slightly open. Sobbing, I threw myself on to the couch beside her.

The couch immediately changed into a rough white surface, as if it had died. Slowly, feebly, I looked up.

I lay inside a concrete pipe of sufficient bore to allow me to turn my head and peer over my shoulder. In me grew that weary sense of lack of identify that was itself an identification. *Non sum ergo sum.* I lay inside a concrete pipe. By being nothing, I am in everything. Even concrete pipes. I could squirt through the sewers of the world unseen.

Although the aim of this narrative is to preserve a picture of my times rather than myself, how could I present myself except as the scenes in which I was temporarily lodged? Perhaps my skeleton inside me lives a vivid life, seeing the universe in his terms. It gives a man little sense of responsibility to imagine his skeleton may enjoy, in its absurdity, grand thoughts of cosmology and first causes.

So I lay inside my concrete pipe, gradually returning to within the confines of normality. Craning my neck over my shoulder, I saw outside the rear of the shop façades and the builders' materials among which I had walked only a brief while ago. One more hallucination to the bad, I thought ; how many to go before I fell completely into a world of unreality, as the doctors had warned me I might? Moreover, this latest dream left me with a disgust which I could not entirely explain, not even by the death of Justine.

Shaking myself out of a fit of introspection, I realized that Israt and probably other pursuers were doubtless searching the area for me. It behoved me to get away as fast as I could.

Courage had left me. To face going out into the open and possibly getting an incendiary bullet in the face was beyond me. After all, I had my skeleton to consider. Taking the line of least resistance, I crawled on down the pipe.

It grew dark as I progressed, and the circle of light behind me dwindled. Faint intimations of claustrophobia came to me and grew stronger. Still I forced myself on, until I came to something solid. My exploring fingers found metal. I pushed, and a flap opened. Light poured in on me. Without taking any precautions to conceal myself, I climbed out.

I was in a large and bare room, at the other end of which stood a telephone switchboard. It stood away from the wall and was not connected. Large drums of cable lay everywhere, and a clutter of line instruments. I assumed that I had come through a pipe that would eventually contain some of the cable.

Nobody was about. I guessed that as it was midday everyone was resting until the heat grew less. A door was open on the other side of the room; I walked out of it and down a corridor. I passed a black woman in a white skirt who looked surprised to see me. "Good morning," I said, and passed on. Unmolested, I walked out of a swing door into the street.

As I went, looking for somewhere that offered something better than a temporary refuge, I discovered what an outlandish place Walvis Bay was.

The city had been planned on the most grandiose scale, and executed on a meagre one. Masses of narrow streets, which were often cul-de-sacs looking rather like mews, clustered together, and then gave out on to a couple of squares with shops and cafés and places of entertainment. These units seemed part of larger units, with main avenues cutting them and a stretch of park and a pool with giant white buildings facing it. But so much was unfinished, the houses with no more than their foundations laid, the shops empty even of fittings, the pools innocent of water, the young trees dying as surely as the trees in my dream. Some buildings – the large ones in particular – seemed to have been built some while past, and these showed cracks across their surface or were actually falling down. In some places, chunks of their façades lay in the street. The shadows lay heavy and black at the feet of these structures, and nobody moved in them.

To me, a hunted man, it seemed like a citadel of death. I wished only to escape from it, and wondered how that could be done. Perhaps I might hire or steal a boat and sail down the coast. With this in mind, I tried to find my way back towards the sea-front. I had lost my direction, but since Walvis Bay was built on a symmetrical pattern, it was not long before I saw the ocean gleaming down the far end of an avenue.

I made towards it, only to find that before I could reach it

I would have to cross what was obviously a main square, a vast and potentially fine place with many grand buildings and, in the middle, a formal garden which had still to be laid out; huge marble plinths stood empty in it, waiting for statues yet to arrive. I saw that the name of this square was President's Square. One of the flanking buildings was evidently a temple. It was finished, at least on the outside. Easily dominating the other buildings, it sent a tall spire up into the blazing sky.

The temple itself, and particularly its tower, were covered in elaborate mosaic. Some of this mosaic work, which at first glance I mistook for a cracked and sun-blistered surface, represented different peoples of Africa, looking out across the seas with proud eyes and nostrils. This elaboration was in such contrast with the severe white stone structures that formed the rest of the square, that I thought of Thunderpeck in his tub on the ship, the elaborate wrinkling of his face conflicting with the blank slopes of his body.

As soon as I saw it, I felt sure that this was the spire I had seen first from the deck of the *Trieste Star*. Several men were working in the great square below it, laying an elaborate array of coloured blocks which would eventually form a pattern covering most of the centre of it.

I could not cross here without exposing myself to danger. Even as I hesitated, the noise of a motor-car reached my ears, sounding from the direction in which I had come. I shrank into the shade of a colonnade that formed part of one of the buildings and looked that way.

A black car radiator glided into sight. Someone was hanging out of the window, scanning side alleys as he moved slowly by. That would be Israt.

The building whose colonnade I sheltered in was another of the monstrous hotels that formed so prominent a part of the city. Without hesitation, I turned and walked into it, working my way through a lounge and away from the windows. As I skirted the reception desk, avoiding the eye of the fellow dozing there, a notice caught my gaze. It drew me up sharp, and then I turned towards the lift, a new purpose in me.

This was the South Atlantic Hotel, where Peter Mercator lived.

CHAPTER EIGHT

THE psychology of the chase is a strange one. It rests on the assumption of a certain attitude of mind in the pursued. I was running because I ran. The sudden shock of finding myself in the very place I had run from brought me up with a jerk and made me realize that my attitude was a false one.

For what in fact had I to fear from Peter Mercator, whoever he was, however mighty he was? I had only to explain to him my identity and how I had come by the letters which had been written to him by Justine. Even at the time, I realized that it might not be quite as easy as that, but certainly it was useless to run round a city where I was without resources. My best plan while I had the element of surprise in my hands, I decided, was the confront the man Mercator and see what I could do to better my and Justine's position.

As I formed this plan, so much at variance with what I had intended a few minutes before, something that my old rag-and-bone mentor and tormentor Jordill said came back to me: "Other people don't decide what you are; they have to act on what you have decided you are." It's a half-truth, but as fruitful as many a whole truth.

Stepping out of the lift on the top floor, I found myself opposite a sumptuous restaurant – or it would be sumptuous when it was completed; one end was a riot of gay murals and elegant tables laid with shining silver and white linen and lustrous heavy crimson roses – but they could not be real in these days! – while the other end showed naked plaster walls and objects shrouded in sheets. This I report now; at the time it was not the sight but the smell that hit me. I stood there realizing how hungry I was.

Four men pushed arrogantly past me. One was half white, the rest black. The half-caste was a shrunken husk of a man, and wore an anti-gravity unit to support him like the one von Vanderhoot had worn. All four were finely dressed, with heavy rings on their fingers, and had about them an air of authority. They passed into the restaurant talking, and went through into a men's room; when they emerged a minute later, the half-caste had removed his unit, and his friends their light coats and furled umbrellas; he was helped to a chair as they arranged themselves at a table. By their deference to him, he was someone of importance.

I walked through the restaurant into the men's room. It was deserted. On a row of hooks hung the old man's antigravity unit, two light coats, and four furled umbrellas. Only the coats interested me. Hastily, I searched their pockets.

They yielded a pair of dark glasses and a cloth wallet in which a stack of notes was rolled. An address written on the wallet indicated that its owner came from the Republic of Algeria and was of ministerial rank. I knew enough about the world situation to understand that Algeria and New Angola were at present hostile towards each other. Much I cared then, as I stuffed the money into my pocket and put the glasses on my nose. I had hoped to find a gun; but the money alone improved my morale.

I would dearly have loved to stop for a meal. The four Africans were settling down to a lengthy feed, by the look of it, but I kept on walking, out into the corridor.

Not knowing where to find Mercator, I paused uncertainly outside.

Down one end of the corridor, a robot plasterer was working. Sometimes these automatons are given communication circuits, sometimes not. This one had a large "Made in Egypt" stamped on its shoulder, so I was hopeful, for Egypt had become the most advanced African state in recent years and her machine products were supposed to be efficient. I asked the thing if it knew where Mercator's suite was, but it did not reply; possibly it was wired for a language other than English.

Near it hung a human decorator's coat. On a sudden inspiration I took it up and put it on, for someone was coming along the adjoining corridor. I had lost my fez long ago, perhaps in the scramble through the concrete pipe. Picking up an empty bucket, I walked away. With the dark glasses on my nose, I felt well disguised. As I turned the corner, I saw that coming towards me was Israt; in front of him walked Doctor Thunderpeck.

Two things were immediately clear: that my old friend was captive, and that he recognized me while Israt didn't. And why should Israt look twice at me, in a building presumably swarming with decorators in white smocks?

I walked past them, swinging my bucket. As soon as I was past Israt, I swung the bucket harder and brought it down round the back of his head. Thunderpeck had the nearest door open, and we dragged him in there. It was a suite, the decoration finished but the furniture not yet in. We spread the tall man out on the floor, and Thunderpeck stood over him with his gun, which Israt had conveniently dropped. He was not laid out cold, but was pretty groggy. I took the dark glasses off and wiped my face.

"You certainly appeared at a convenient time," Thunderpeck said. "How are you bearing under the strain? Let me feel your pulse rate."

I gave him my wrist. He took hold of it without removing his gaze from Israt.

"You'll survive. In fact you'll make a fine corpse. When you left the convoy so promptly, they kept me covered and did an abortive tour of the city trying to pick you up again. They must be used to dealing with imbeciles, the way they let you get away."

"Where was Israt taking you?"

"Why, to this chap Mercator, who seems to be the king-pin round here."

"Good. We'll go and see him together. This matter can all be easily sorted out. Where's Justine?"

"She's somewhere in the building. She left me downstairs. Take my advice, forget her – she's a dangerous woman, Knowle. Best thing we could do is to get out of here. I don't want to meet Mercator. The way things have turned out, we'd have done better with the New Angolese. These are desperate men here."

"I must get this thing sorted out, Doc. For Justine, if not for me. If you want to go off on your own, that's all right with me."

"Now you're being silly."

I slapped him on the shoulder and squatted down to speak to Israt, who was propping himself up on one elbow and staring muzzily at us.

"Look, friend, the honours are even between us," I told him. "You nearly killed me with an incendiary gun, I clobbered you with a bucket. So let's have no evil thoughts about one another. Instead, how about some answers to some questions? First of all, whereabouts is your boss, Mercator? Is he up on this floor?"

Israt was a sensible fellow. With his eyes on his own gun in Thunderpeck's hand, he said: "We are going there. Mr. Mercator's suite is round the corner to the left."

"Opposite the restaurant?"

"Yes. Next to the elevator."

"Good. Next question. Who was von Vanderhoot?"

"Von Vanderhoot was Mr. Mercator's secretary. We discovered too late that he was in the pay of the Prime Minister of Algeria, General Ramayanner Kurdan, a very dangerous man. By then, von Vanderhoot had disappeared with some important documents – letters. This was yesterday. I was seeking for him in New Angola territory when I found you. You are von Vanderhoot's agent."

"Leaving that aside, why should von Vanderhoot be thought to have disappeared into New Angola if he was an agent for Algeria, when Algeria is supposed to be an enemy of New Angola?"

Israt shrugged and looked contemptuous.

"Because, my clever man, the contents of those letters we found on you are as damaging to Mr. Mercator in the one state as the other. Von Vanderhoot was paid to make trouble for us. Don't pretend you do not know that both states are particularly interested in Walvis Bay in this historic week."

This was getting beyond me.

"Israt, I swear I am innocently involved in all this. What in particular is happening in Walvis Bay this week?"

"You make fools of us both, Mr. Noland, to make me repeat to you information you have long ago. This city is specially built on specially ceded land that belongs to none of the African states. There has been big argument over it since the twentieth century, but it is independent territory. Now it is used by the United African Nations, at the inspiration of President el Mahasset, to build a great sea-coast resort where all of Africa can meet on neutral territory and enjoy themselves. It is the greatest practical move ever made to unite our continent in reality and not just in name. And although a thousand enemies have delayed its building and sabotaged every step of progress, Walvis Bay will be officially opened tomorrow by President el Mahasset himself, for the greater glory of Africa, although it is not really finished and only a few guests are here. The world press and representatives of all nations are already pouring in ; and that, as you know, is why – tomorrow will be the greatest day in Africa's history!"

I stood up. Thunderpeck and I looked at each other.

"I never enjoy greatest days," I said. "Doc, can you stay here and guard Israt, while I go along and see Mercator? If I'm not back in half an hour, you'd better tie this fellow up and get away as best you can."

"For God's sake, Knowle, we don't know this place! Where can we arrange to meet?"

In his ear I said, so that Israt should not hear: "Outside this hotel is the biggest square in the city, President's Square. The biggest building looking on to it has the tallest tower. Nobody could miss that. It's a sort of temple. I will meet you there if we get split up – at the base of the tower."

He shook his head. "Mad," he said. He was still shaking his head as I walked out of the room.

I walked down the corridor in my white smock and dark glasses. As I went, I tried to assimilate what Israt had told us. What I had regarded as a city of despair was in fact a city of hope. That in itself would be enough to attract the vultures. I could imagine them clearly without having to be told about them: shabby little cliques with business interests, politicians with axes to grind, thugs who stood to gain by a divided Africa. Unconsciously, I began to allot a role to Mercator.

After I had turned left down the corridor, I found myself before a door on which stood a small card bearing three words: PETER MERCATOR, ENGLAND. Looking uneasily round, I saw the four men I had robbed still feeding and drinking in the restaurant. No doubt they were some of the visiting dignitaries, here for the opening of Walvis Bay, or the grinding of a special axe. I thought what an old injustice it was, as old as man, that they should live so vilely well while the people they were supposed to represent languished in the confines of their lives on half-rations.

When I knocked on Mercator's door, a firm voice said: "Come in."

Entering, I found myself in a small hall with several doors leading off it. One of them was open. I glimpsed a room with a balcony and a view of sea and promenade. Sitting on the arm of a chair was a small neat man. Hypnotized, I went towards him.

His hair was white, his face pallid, his eyebrows and goatee black, though streaked with grey. Though I had seen him only once in my life before, I could never forget that face.

"Peter Mercator?" I asked.

"Yes, come in," said the Farmer.

CHAPTER NINE

In my boyhood, Hammer and I used to play Farmers and Landsmen. Or it would be Farmers and Travellers or Farmers and Citymen, but always Farmers and something. As small boys, we understood Farmers; they were big and powerful and cruel, as we longed to be while we went on our grimy tasks for our master.

Farmers had the right to pursue. Farmers could beat. Although Hammer and I were much of a match when it came to running or to pitting puny muscle against muscle, when one of us played Farmer, he came the stronger. Under the mantle of that terrible title, the one became the superior of the other – even of the Traveller. So much is in a name. The rotten young teeth in our mouths grew white again when we became, briefly, Farmers.

Of course, neither of us knew what Farmer properly was, or what he did. But we knew that life in the platform cities depended on the Farmers; because they held the food for the mouths of the people, they also held the knife at their throats. Because the Farmer was a shadowy figure, he was the more terrifying. We saw people dying from various sophisticated nutritional ills, or from brute starvation, and we blamed the Farmers.

Hammer and I were as subtle as a cement wall. We had no learning, and an intelligence as narrow and sharp as a knife. At night beneath our blankets, our dreams were ashy fires burning in caves.

That one day I remember when I played the Farmer. Inside me, all the cruelties gave me strength, yet I could not capture Hammer. He was playing one of the Travellers. We pictured those men as wearing bright rags, seven feet tall, with a mane of hair hanging over their cats' eyes, and the swaggering postures that they used for freedom.

Traveller Hammer catapulted up the weary side streets of the Shuttered Quarter, suddenly swinging into side alleys, lying by broken walls till I passed, whooping back on his tracks, kicking himself round corners, sometimes with my hand poised above – but never quite closing on – his shaggy collar. Because of some special sickness that had swept this part of the city several seasons past, it has been boarded up and was deserted, despite the fearful crowding in the rest of the city.

Officially it was deserted. The human rat lived everywhere in the city, the thinnest plank sheltered him. We had found our way through the boards. So had many other humans, the real Unspeakables of the city, who now shacked up here against the mud and dust of that winter. In fact, our errand for our master lay with these people, and we had traded his rags in the Shuttered Quarter at a price to his advantage. Our grimy game of Farmer celebrated the deal.

Clattering round a corner went Hammer, into a walled yard. The wall at the far end was no higher than his chest, but I saw he was too winded to climb it. He sprawled in a corner, gasping.

A sort of hut was there, built of some old bricks and boxes, and with a warped plastic sheet for roof, secured into place with stones. From this dwelling had come a man. He now leant shuddering against the low wall, and we watched him die.

He had the Flakers, as it was known – some sort of a flesh disease. Neither Hammer nor I had seen its effects before. The man vibrated considerably, and went into a sort of hopping dance. As he did so, he pulled off the remnants of his clothes. At the same time, pieces of his flesh fell off, for all the world like bits of rag. I seem to remember that his cheeks went first.

There was little blood, just these falling leaves in the sudden autumn of his flesh.

We couldn't help it. Together we burst into laughter. It was a wonderful sight, made the funnier because the man paid no attention to us. He went on doing that funny dance, which at first we imitated; but the comedy of it was too much, and soon we were forced just to watch. As the man sank down on to his threadbare knees, someone threw a stone at us.

A woman crouched in the entrance to the improvised hut. You would not have thought the little place could have housed two of them. We ran more from her face than from the stone she threw. Her face was stretched so long it had teeth and darkness in it. Only when we were out of the yard did we dare to laugh again.

Through the city we went, our game of Farmer forgotten. It was time to go home. We put arms round each other's shoulders, partly from affection, partly to keep together in the mob of people pressing along once we got free of the Shuttered Quarter. Of traffic, there was only the occasional public vehicle. Everything else that was mechanical and had to move, moved under the surface of the city, in the service-ways. But the people – a throng, composed of separate bodies, of groups, of processions, pushing this way and that – the people devoured the street space.

Some people walked with intent, some with the shuffle that denotes no purpose or no destination. When you can find no work, you can find no money to pay for rooms; then you are turned into the street, where you can be arrested for vagrancy. But when you find work – the successful housing of yourself and your family into one room drives you to madness, to suffocation, to boredom, to quarrels, and to the streets once more. Married couples take to sleeping by turn in the rooms while the other partner walks outside. That way they get peace, and avoid begetting. And walking can be a substitute for hunger, the tiredness of the legs overcoming the pinch of the intestines. It deadens anxious nerves, and brings a slinking peace of mind. It is an entertainment, a way of life, a sort of death.

"There is no future for our generations," said March Jordill. "Below a certain living level, there is nothing for the individual but today. The power to speculate and plan ahead were hard won; the human race grasped that power only for a brief while before letting it slip away. When you don't think

85

about tomorrow, you see no contradiction in raising a large family to starve and cause you to starve. The poor have inherited the world and beat it about the head with their stringy untiring reproductive organ." March Jordill, the Ragman, was my master, and Hammer's.

We forced our way back to his place, through the rogues and Unspeakables. Some streets were being widened, to provide a better thoroughfare for the population. Some were being narrowed, to provide extra rooms for the population.

March Jordill's was a gaunt house, containing offices of tiny companies – the Megapole Sickness Fund, United Milk Water Stiffener Company, Preghast Associates, Human Water Development Finance, Breeze Fumigation Company, Parallax Birth-Death Bidders, Unclepox – where the directors and secretaries slept, dreaming of their luck, under the desks, come nightfall – with the March Jordill Rags Co. on the top floor, its sagging roof pointing towards the still unpopulated stars. That top floor was the first home I had known.

Hammer had been sold into apprenticeship to Jordill; I had been given to him from the orphanage. We knew we were in luck. March Jordill was mad. To work for a sane man was disaster in the grinding survival conditions of the city. And we were lucky that the Human Water Development Finance lay so near. We saved our water, precious and golden, never letting a drop go astray, leaking it into containers, to get the pittance per gallon it would fetch in the offices below us. A week's leak made us millionaires compared with many of the other young ruffians we knew along the street.

My master was found on the roof, where he liked to go when there was no business in the musty rooms below, lolling and talking to the broken-nosed widow woman Lamb who performed many tasks for him, from the most casual to the most awful and intimate, perhaps in the hope that he would marry her and raise her above her official Unspeakable statue.

As we went round to him, Jordill gripped us and looked us up and down. Half his face, the lower half, was all but empty. Into the upper half were crowded all the hair left to him, the furrows that marked his brow, his eyebrows, his deep eyes in their tuckers of flesh, his blunt brief nose with its tip upturned rudely towards the world. In the lower half, set above the blank spade of his chin, lay the neat divide of his mouth. That mouth, almost lipless, opened and shut like a sort of fly-trapping plant when he spoke.

"So you boys have escaped the combined stewpots of the city's rascals, and are back to me again – with a handsome profit, I hope?" he said.

Hammer had not the same respect for our master that I held. He struggled out of his grip and stood back.

"We got what you told us," he said.

"I expected no less of you, boy. Hand it over, then."

"I've got it, Master," I said. From under the tunic that covered my ribs, I pulled the little ornament that the people of the Shuttered Quarter had given me in exchange for the rags we had taken them. I would have given it to the master, but he snatched it from me and held it aloft, laughing from his pale mouth, so that his chin and head tipped different ways. He threw it to the widow woman Lamb, who caught it neatly and held it between her eyes and the sky, making a ticking noise with her tongue as she did so.

"One of them!" she said.

"Worth a bit when melted down, worth more when sold to the Manskin Believers!"

"There aren't none of them left!" exclaimed old Lamb, shocked by the mention of this outlaw creed. "They was all routed out by the police and sent for landsmen long ago, back before Jack died."

"I know better – as usual I know better," March Jordill said, splitting his face with another laugh. "Nothing is ever eradicated, Lambkin, no shred of clothing, no weed, no sin, no hope. The Manskins are cleverer now, and do their snatching in more devious ways, but their belief has died no more than they, and once we contact them with this nice idol of their faith, they'll pay handsomely."

"Master March, it's illegal, and I fear for you –"

They went into one of their arguments that I did not attempt to follow. Hammer slipped away, scowling because I would not join him. But I stood long hours not understanding a tenth of what March Jordill said in order to grasp a little, and now that I was growing older I understood more. Now I gathered from his conversation that this ornament we had carried back for him from the Shuttered Quarter was in fact an image of a forbidden cult, of which there were many in the teeming byways near us.

This idol of the Manskin cult was a bare ugly thing with two male faces, one on its head, one on its chest. Its feet stood apart, its buttocks were braced, it clenched its fists against its metal shoulders. Although I did not like it, I did not dare laugh at it.

"Don't understand it all, at all," old Lamb said, making the wry face that usually went with her shaken head. "In my young days there wasn't all this trouble, everyone believing something different."

"Ah, you're wrong there," March Jordill said with relish, for he loved to emphasize other people's wrongness. "Everyone has begun to believe the same again, now that human self-consciousness is sinking back into mass consciousness. We're witnessing the belief in only one thing, though it comes superficially disguised in many forms – the belief in the animal darkness from which we rose so comparatively short a time ago. Over-population has not only brought a collapse of economic organization, which is and always was dependent on agricultural organization, but a collapse in mental organization. We're all animists again. This compulsively vile little idol –"

"It's all very well you talking, but I don't see why people shouldn't have as many children as they want. It's the only right that hasn't been taken away from them, heaven knows." Old Lamb always grew heated on this subject, having borne fifteen children herself. "I know what's to blame! It isn't nobody's fault here, it's the fault of these African states you hear about. They don't help anybody, they just go on fighting each other and don't bother about us in the poorer nations. People say to me, Why should they bother about us? but *I* say, we're human same as them, aren't we? Why shouldn't a white man be as good as a black man, I say. I tell 'em! I'm used to speaking out straight, ah, and in language as anyone can understand, not this high-flown stuff you gets out of them old books. I used to speak out straight to Jack and all. I never stood any nonsense from any man –"

"You must have stood a good deal to have been so prodigal of progeny," Jordill observed. "But don't you see the emergence of the African nations is the consequence of our downfall, not its cause. Alas, the demise of the historic sense! In one part of the world after another, man has outrun his natural resources, simply because he will not curb his natural tendencies at the same time as he curbs his natural enemies. The Middle East, the East, became impoverished and worn out, then Europe, then America and the Usser. So the nations withered and collapsed, until now there remains no power but the African states. The topsoil there – in many regions – is still rich enough to support a pugnacious and *aware* set of nations. That situation won't last, of course. Unless something radical happens pretty fast, we shall then see the end of mankind. But look at the rabble flocking down in the street! You think they care?"

"Well, I don't know about that, but I used to say to Jack before he got himself trampled to death in that riot, 'Jack,' I said, 'you may be bigger than me, but that's a fact you haven't got half so much sense as me, worshipping these strange religions, if you'd call them that.' He became an Abstainer for a brief period, right when it wasn't fashionable, as certain people seem to think it is now – you know, didn't want to lie with me or anything like that. O' course, being a man, he couldn't keep that up for long."

"Even in its happiest historical period, the intellect was never a very certain ruler of the body. . . ."

So their talk would flow on, while I stood there slack-mouthed, listening. I was not only puzzled by what March Jordill said, but by the way he said it, for in these conversations it was as if he worked himself into the part of a seer, and spoke in an ornate (what I learnt through reading to know as a literary) manner; the more he adopted this fashion, the less likely old Lamb was to understand him; and so I came to realize that he was talking mainly for his own benefit. It was only much later, when I was a convict and had the leisure of thought permitted to a landsman, that it struck me that in this my master was no different from old Lamb herself, or from countless others I met. Even the old books I found: had their authors gone to their great trouble in order to communicate with other people or to commune with themselves? Thus I arrived at a picture of my world, where all were so assailed by others that in defence they turned in towards their own selves. Once I believed that this was the only piece

89

of knowledge I possessed not owned by March Jordill. Now I do not even know if it is knowledge.

My master ended this strange conversation when the old widow burst into belated tears to recall the death of her husband in the riots. Jordill rose, turned his back on her weeping, placed the Manskin idol on the parapet that ran round the roof, and looked down at the mobs in the street below. Then he chanted at them, words I had heard from him before so often that I had them memorized, though he changed them or rearranged them at will.

> "Gaze at each other, people!
> You should not have stopped your looking
> People of people, like unwatched topiary
> You grow unlikely shapes
> Out of the bulworks of you birthworks
> From the multitudinous bums
> Of your gods, no eye regards you –
> Look to yourselves, Earth's peoples, Earthworks!
> Look, look hard, and take a knife,
> Carve yourself a conscience!"

The words went to the winds, and before they were done, a knocking from below summoned us. He slipped the idol into one of his voluminous patch pockets, lay a hand commandingly on my shoulder, and we climbed below, to meet a customer with whom my master went into a long haggle.

Our room was full of the clutter of our trade – not only old clothes of every description, but any other objects that my master had acquired with the idea of getting a good price for later. There were things here from the past for which the present, I thought, could have no use. They gave me a strange feeling about the past; I had a picture of lonely people doing and wanting strange things that were irrelevant to the real and important matters of life. From the books this impression came with particular strength. There were many books, for nobody wanted them in a city where nobody could read, books piled into old boxes or heaped in one corner to make a sort of table at which old Lamb worked a sewing-machine. Because my master was mad, he would read these books, aloud sometimes, much to Hammer's disgust, for he did not at all understand the principle of reading. I understood, and March Jordill encouraged me.

"Cutting off, boy, cutting off," he said to me, his eyes staring over their little rought embankments of flesh. "That's been the way of man all along, and it's been the wrong way. Somewhere, something fatal went wrong with the pattern – but we won't go into that. What I'm telling you is that we only got where we are by cutting ourselves off from the world about us. Do you know the biggest advance ever made by our hairless tribe?"

"Discovering the wheel?" That was something I'd read about, and even as I piped the question the notion was in my head that somewhere in the maze of the city that wheel might still be found, vast and aged and wormy-wooden, if one looked diligently enough: the Original Wheel, as momentous as the Original Sin.

"No, not that, boy. Nor the discovery of fire. Far more vital was the discovery that food could be cooked in the fire, because by so doing those little scrawny men unknowingly cut themselves off from a great deal of disease. There are living things in raw flesh, you see, worms that transfer themselves into your belly and live there when you eat them. They are killed when meat is cooked. That way, a great and perpetual drain on the tribe's health – mental as well as physical health, since the two cannot but go together – was wiped out. And the tribe that first took to cooking was the only sort of animal with that advantage. Because they ate better, they lived better in every way, and that was how man got the edge on all the other animals."

"We don't eat very well now, master. I'm hungry as anything."

"We don't live very well now! That's what's wrong with the world. We may have killed off all the dangerous animals, but we have eaten and copulated ourselves out of our inheritance, see. . . . But what was I saying?"

If you did not give him his cue, he became very angry, and would strike us, which was why Hammer didn't care much for him. "You were saying someone cut themselves, master."

"No, I wasn't. I was saying how people cut themselves off, and I was giving you an instance." He screwed his eyes up and looked with his head held sideways at a pile of trouser legs. "People progressed by cutting themselves off from the natural world. But now they's taken it a stage further. When the soil grew so foul, they moved the cities on to raised platforms to cut themselves off from it, but that cut them off from their own past as well. That's why everything's gone to pot. We're cut off from the wisdom of the ages."

"I thought you said it was to do with – having too many people?" He produced a thousand reasons for the state of the world, a new one with almost every book he managed to read, and I was confused. But he took me by the shoulders and shook me and laughed his split-faced laugh and said: "If you live to be a man, you'll make a good arguer. Always listen to arguments, boy – sometimes there's a grain of truth in them."

Sometimes he seemed to treat me as if he thought I mattered. At other times, he growled that he was surrounded by fools like me and old Lamb and Hammer. Now that he was occupied with a customer, I crawled under the table and got under my blanket beside Hammer. March Jordill slept on top of the table, on a thick arrangement of wadding and pillows, for he suffered badly in his limbs from sciatic and other pains, so that sometimes we were scared by his groaning. The smell under the table was cosy and ripe, and we lay there against each other to keep out the cold, listening to the haggle with half an ear.

No conclusion was come to, for my master's customer was clearly asking for the impossible. At last, my master showed the man to the door that led down the stairs to the street, and opened it.

A black-uniformed policeman came in, levelling a weapon at my master.

At the same time – we could see it from where we crouched – the door from the roof swung open, and another patroller appeared with a prison robot behind him. They must have been landed on the roof by whirleycab, and while the argument was going on we had not heard them.

March Jordill turned and saw he was trapped. His face went very white and old. It was funny: for the first time in my life, I realized that he was not a very old man, as I had hitherto thought of him, but a young man who was just all old on the inside. His limbs began to shake, almost like the man whose flesh we had watched fall off.

"What do you want?" he asked.

"March Jordill, you are charged with illegal trading on seventeen different counts," one of the patrollers said. "You will come with us."

"I want to hear the charges before I move from here," my master said.

Boredly, the patroller brought out a little speaker and switched it on. It announced the seventeen charges, all of which Hammer and I recognized; they did not mention the Manskin idol, or any number of other deals, but I knew it was enough to get March Jordill shipped as a landsman for life.

Some mad ideas of helping him ran into my mind. I was going to jump out and shout at the cops, but before I could move, Hammer grabbed my shoulder and pulled me back into the darkness by him. He put a hand lightly over my mouth to show me that we must not speak or breathe.

My master was put into the prison robot. These things were legged and tracked devices, shaped roughly like a man; they opened up, and there was room for one person to be enclosed inside. The robot could then move under its own power, and take the person away for questioning in the police headquarters below the city.

And that's what happened. In a minute, all the party was gone. I lay there absolutely stunned.

"Come on, grumble guts, we're got to get out of here before they come back and search the place," Hammer said, scrambling over me and climbing from under the table. "They'll send us to the land just because we work for old Jordill. Get moving!"

I climbed out and stood staring at him miserably.

"You go," I said.

"Too true I'm going – and if you've got any sense, you'll get sparking too, Orphanage!" He was running round wildly. He had seized a clothes bag, and was stuffing various articles of value into it. I saw that March Jordill had stood the Manskin idol on a side ledge during his argument with the difficult customer (who had no doubt been planted by the patrollers); Hammer seized the idol and pushed it into his bag.

At the door, he paused and regarded me.

"Coming, Knowle?"

"Soon, I suppose."

"Shake out of it, patient! The old boy's gone for good, you know that. See me – right from now, I'm free and grown up. I'm going to make my own way. Why not come along?"

"Not yet."

"Thumbs, then!" Lifting his thumb in salute, he left, the bag slung across one shoulder.

There was nothing in me. I went over to the dusty window and peered out. In a minute, Hammer appeared under the dim street lamp, for it was now dusk. As he stepped into the street, a uniformed man who had been watching the building came out of the shadows and grabbed him by the arm, twisting it and marching him off. Thus ended Hammer's period of being free and grown up.

Now it was safe for me to make a getaway. But before leaving I stood there in tears, the first I had shed since orphanage days, tears for my solitude, tears for the darkness coming in like sludge, tears for my master, having his long and clever head punched far below, tears for things I would never know.

When, several years later, I became a landsman myself, I met Hammer again, now a guard, rough, crude, surviving. Throughout the years, I hoped that I would meet March Jordill again. It never happened. Instead, I found myself confronting, one particular hot day in Walvis Bay, the man called Peter Mercator, whom I had long known and loathed as "The Farmer".

CHAPTER TEN

THE surprise robbed me of the disadvantage I had. Yet perhaps what I did then surprised him more than anything else I could have thought of. I took off my dark glasses, folded them into a pocket, and said simply: "I'm Knowle Noland. You wanted to speak to me."

He got up and came forward. With his white hair and black eyebrows, his face was very striking. I saw his eyes active under the eyebrows, searching me, summing me up.

"Certainly I want to speak to you. Let's go and sit down over by the window."

As I walked into the room, I saw that he had another man with him, a small and old man with a flabby face and restless hands that sought each other's company. From his clothes and businesslike air, I guessed he was a professional man rather than a gunman – I was on the watch for trouble.

Mercator confirmed my guess by turning to the little man and saying: "I'd like you to leave us for a while, Doctor."

The doctor hesitated. "Remember what I say. Drugs aren't everything. You must rest more, or I won't answer for the consequences."

With quiet desperation (was it that?) Mercator said: "In two days' time, Doctor, I will try to do as you bid, if we are still here."

At that the doctor bowed stiffly and withdrew.

From the cushioned seats by the window, I could see down through the venetian blinds on to the promenade. In the brilliant afternoon's sun, several people were strolling there, and I thought the place looked to be growing more crowded. It was a long way to the ground; I had forgotten for a while that this hotel room was seventeen storeys up.

"You are causing me a little trouble, Mr. Noland," Mercator said, seating himself so that he could scrutinize me as he had once done in an anonymous office, many years earlier. "I have no idea what whim drove you to walk in here like this, but I cannot allow you to walk out again a free man, at least until tomorrow night, when the fireworks are over and I am on my way back to England."

"I have come to explain how innocently I am involved in your affairs. What you are doing here is of no interest to me, except in as much as it concerns Justine Smith."

He raised an eyebrow, saying almost wistfully: "Justine. . . ."

"Yes, Justine – your mistress!"

His face was more haggard than I recalled it. In the way he held himself, too, he looked not only older but ill. Deep lines ran down from his nose to his jaw. The lines accentuated themselves now as he said: "Certainly I am prepared to believe that you know very little about my organization if you believe that. Justine is not, in the sense you mean it, my mistress ; nor could she be. She is a virgin. And in that sense, I also am a virgin."

Angrily, I said: "You needn't try to be funny."

"I suppose you may find it funny, for I observe you are a pleb, but I am speaking of a matter of personal conviction; and on that conviction rests this present perilous enterprise. Justine!"

He called, and Justine herself came through from a side room. She looked as beautiful and as cool as ever. Her cheekbones, I noticed for the first time, were high, with shadows under them ; and I wondered, with a flush of love, what nationality, or what mixture of nationalities, she might be. She went and stood by Mercator, who had risen, without touching him.

"Mr. Noland has called on us, Justine."

"I told you he promised to do so."

"Justine!" I exclaimed. "You remember what I said to you – and you told me that you were Mercator's prisoner. You lied to me!"

She said, frowning slightly: "You are very far from understanding this situation in which you flounder. Nor is it true that I told you I was Peter's prisoner. If I said I was a prisoner, I was speaking metaphorically and meant merely a prisoner of necessity. What are we going to do with him, Peter?"

The glance they gave each other! Though both looked sick and harassed, there was complete trust in that look, a trust that inevitably excluded me, and I could not bear to see it.

I jumped up and faced Mercator.

"You do not recognize me," I told him. "Why should you? We met only briefly many years ago, and then I was so stunned by long imprisonment and interrogation that to you I was just one of the many miserable landsmen dragged before you! To me you were then the Farmer, and I was too lowly even to know your real name. Now I am before you again, and in my right mind, and am not going to be fobbed off with the spoonful of scorn I was before!"

He sat down again. He put his brow against his hand, resting his elbow on his knee.

"How often I dreamed that nemesis would take the shape of a landsman. ..." he said, mainly to himself. "Noland, Noland ... yes, weren't you the man who gave evidence about the Traveller, Gipsy Jess?"

After all those years, my face burnt at the mention of that disgraceful night. Reading the affirmative he sought, Mercator continued: "And did you really think I treated you with scorn? Why, I did what I could for you! I saved you from the police cells. Didn't I get you some sort of job?"

"You got me on to the *Trieste Star* as a bit of super-numerary human crew. I worked my way up to Captain long after you had forgotten all about me. I've come here to tell you that yesterday I had the pleasure of piling up that rotten ship of yours on to the shore not a dozen miles from here!"

He shook his head, looking at Justine as if for sympathy as he answered me. "I sold my interest in the Star Line freighters five years ago; most of my capital these days is tied up in the anti-gravity industry. That's the up-and-coming thing; if you've saved any money, Noland, I'd advise you to put it in anti-gravity. Unless there's a world war, of course."

At that, he and Justine smiled wearily at each other.

"I'm offering the advice now, Mercator — I've suffered too much from you in the past."

He rose and said: "I've no interest in past suffering. I'm too occupied with the present. I can't let you go out of here, Noland. You obviously have a chip on your shoulder and aren't entirely responsible for your own actions. Would you like a drink, and perhaps you'll be good enough to tell me how you got mixed up with von Vanderhoot?"

Let me not say here how I hated this man who lived so easily, who enjoyed his power so easily, who turned aside my wrath so easily. Not only did I loathe what I thought was his attitude to life — I envied all the things and qualities he had that I had never found myself heir to.

"I'm explaining nothing, Mercator — kill me if you will. I told Justine what little I know and I'm not repeating myself. No doubt she repeated it to you. Nor will I have a drink with you." Even as I spoke, to my added fury, my stomach rumbled loudly, reminding me how hungry I was.

He walked over to a cabinet and poured drinks for himself and Justine. Though he said nothing more, I saw with satisfaction that his hand trembled. Justine stood looking down at me. I could not interpret her dark gaze; my rough life had brought me nobody like Justine.

She said quietly: "You behave so strangely. You are ill in

some sort of way, aren't you? Would it help you if you understood what we are doing here?"

I burst into angry laughter.

"It's a pleasure to hear you talk, Justine, whatever you say!"

She turned and walked into the next room. Mercator gave her a warning glance and a shake of the head, but she ignored him. I followed her. Mercator came meekly enough after her, handed her a drink in a slender glass and went out again, though he left the door open behind him.

Her voice when she spoke was low and conspiratorial. It was also husky with accusation. How hard it is to bear the contempt of a beautiful woman, even when your stomach grumbles its emptiness aloud!

"You are impossible with him, Knowle! Try – try and use some understanding of how others feel. Peter is a proud man, just like you – how can you expect any sort of agreement between you when you can speak to him the way you do?"

"Agreement? I can reach no agreement with him! He's one of the men who have made my life a misery. But for him, I'd be –"

"You're making feeble excuses. I heard you in there! Really, Knowle, I took you for something better. Have you no creed? Have your relations with other people always been such a mess?"

All the knocks I have received in times past do not rankle as much as did those words. I did not then know how she condemned me from her particular narrow religious viewpoint, as I had no idea of her beliefs apart from the hint Mercator had dropped; but I felt immediately that her barb came poisoned with truth: my relationships with others mainly ended in failure or betrayal. What surer signpost is there to the failure of one's own personality?

Now, at a maturer age, I can see that the health of character is securely tied to the health of an age; dissolution produces dissolution, betrayal betrayal, and trust is no neighbour for fear. But at that time, I still nourished a belief in the idea that personalities shape history, rather than vice versa, and my hurt at Justine's words was the greater.

I remember dropping my eyes and shuffling away from her.

"Keep quiet about it, Justine – that side of it is none of your business. Perhaps you don't know his past. It's men like him who are ruining England, with their awful system of exploiting men and land alike. You would understand nothing about that."

Her manner remained irritatingly patient.

"Don't be condescending. I have been to England, and Peter and I have no secrets from each other – we are both of the same faith."

"Never mind your faith! I'm saying you have no idea of what he did to me personally."

"I know he saved you from the land. He said so, and he never lies. Besides, England is finished, worn out, ruined, just like all the other rotten little states of Europe, yes, and of Russia and China, and what was known as the United States, in which I was born. You know nothing of the world picture – your are just a pleb. Africa is the only place with fight left in it, in its men and territories. Why do you think the other poor tottering countries like yours and mine have made treaties and alliances with the various African States? Why, so that they can get assistance from them – as you were getting sand –"

"Sand! Sand! My God, Justine, there's gnerosity on the African States' part. How good of them to spare England a few holdsfull of their sand! But you know we have to pay for it – and yet they could produce enough from their stinking Skeleton Coast alone to drown all England in sand. I bet your pal next door gets his cut out of the deal somewhere, doesn't he? Tell me what he's doing here if he's not after some financial deal or other."

"We are here for other reasons." Now my words had hurt her. She swung her hand and slapped me across the cheek. "Reasons you would not grasp! Don't you understand how we hate your kind? And aren't your kind with their petty little rightousness – their materialist pride – engulfing the world? Millions upon millions of them, gorging up the earth's supplies with their narrow beliefs!"

Hurt though I was, my pride most of all, I said: "Okay, Justine, you're a little aristocrat and you hate the common people. Your kind has enjoyed the ascendancy throughout most of history. But I'm as good as you. I can read as well as you can, and I'm not so puffed up! My belly rumbles disgustingly in front of you because I'm hungry, yet you can talk about my gorging myself on the world's supplies. That's what *your* kind does!"

She turned on her heel and walked to the far wall.

"Your beliefs and mine are absolutely opposed; I was a fool to argue with you," she said. Her anger had gone the moment she saw me rubbing my cheek. "I did not realize how unreasonable you were. The current régime throughout the world remains almost unchallenged because there is nobody left who holds clear ideas about the nature of man and the universal character of the human condition. It arose because not enough people could command a metaphysical view of human nature. We are spiritually and agriculturally bankrupt – perhaps the two must always go together."

This Justine said rather awkwardly, and it occurred to me that she was parroting something Mercator had said to her. At the same time, there was enough of a defensive note in her voice to suggest she was perhaps trying to offer an explanation for her own touchy behaviour. Sharp desire like sexual longing seized me; I wished to know and understand her. And yet, being contradictory, I refused to let what she had said seem to mollify me.

"I don't understand what you are talking about, and it's irrelevant anyway."

"No doubt you'll find this irrelevant too."

She placed a tape on a turntable; and set it spinning. Voices came forth, and I recognized them. They were voices I had often listened to on board the *Trieste Star,* only to turn them off in boredom. They were the English-speaking radio stations of the various most powerful African States: Algeria, New Angola, Waterberg, West Congo, Egypt, Ghana, Goya, Nigeria. Their world attitude, as I knew, was tough and energetic, and not without its hints of aggression towards Europe and America, or more than a hint towards each other.

"I don't want to hear that bloody stuff!" I shouted, for she kept turning the volume higher.

"Listen to them, Knowle, my tough bully boy – don't they frighten you with their greedy demands?"

"Turn them off, Justine!"

"They sound just like the European nations a couple of

centuries ago, Knowle; did you know that? They all want the same thing – more land!"

"I said I don't want to hear them. Switch 'em off!"

"And you know that only one man can keep them all peaceable together at this time? In this whole continent, only one man has a chance of securing ultimate peace among the African nations – President el Mahasset." Still she turned the volume higher. The thick voices blared out at us, their words by now indistinguishable.

"TURN IT OFF, WOMAN!"

"... AND PETER MERCATOR AND I ARE GOING TO KILL THE PRESIDENT TOMORROW!"

Suddenly I was free from the spell that meeting had thrown over me, and the idea of action returned.

As I sprang to the door, Mercator reached it from the other side. Without pausing to think, I hit him hard on the jaw. While he was still reeling back, I crossed the room and ran out through the hall to the corridor.

Justine's shouted words still raced through my mind They convinced me that she and Mercator were in a conspiracy of madness.

I looked to right and left as I moved past the first corridor junction. To the right, I saw Israt. He was talking to a uniformed man – I took him for police. Israt saw me and shouted. I realized that I had been in Mercator's suite for more than half an hour, and Thunderpeck had gone.

Only for a moment did I hesitate. They were moving towards me, and it prompted my thinking marvellously. I turned into the restaurant. The four dignitaries were still there. They had reached the coffee and brandy stage of their meal, and were grinning widely at each other, except for the half-caste, who sat shrunken in his chair, toying with a glass of water. I nodded to them as I turned into the men's room.

In a minute, Mercator's men would be after me. This time it would be an affair of bullets, not words. These people were here to assassinate the President of Africa! They had told me their mad secret, and I could not be trusted – I was a hated pleb! No doubt Justine, the fair, the fatal, had revealed the truth only out of piqued pride; it was enough that she had told me. I guessed it would seal my fate.

Seizing one of the decorator's planks that lay at the far

side of the room, I wedged it with one end behind the side of a wash-basin and the other behind a hot-air drier, so that it lay across the door, stopping it from opening. That would keep them out for a brief minute; there was no lock on the simple spring door. Crossing to the coats that I had previously robbed, I lifted down the half-caste's anti-gravity kit. At the same time, someone thudded violently against the door.

I saw plaster fall under the wash-basin. Damn them for building so badly! There was no time to adjust the harness and strap the unit on properly. I ran to the window with it hanging from one shoulder, flung the window open, and climbed up on to the sill.

Nausea and extreme panic overtook me immediately, as I saw the streets far below. Remember, I had never tried one of these units before; at that date, they were still novelties. But it was too late to turn back now. The blows at the door came again, and the wash-basin squeaked in its socket. Grasping the starting-knob of the unit, I wrenched it over to the "On" position, and jumped clear of the building.

The streets at once began to whirl up at me. Everything in that instant was presented in extreme clarity. I realized that many people were now filling the streets, I even saw jet liners circling by the horizon, as if bringing in more people for to-morrow's ceremony. And by then some terrible thing invaded my mind; there seemed to be strange smells and odours, and I realized that the unit was not working. I extended my hands, I yelled amid splendid music! Roofs, pavements, whirled up at me – and I hit ground!

CHAPTER ELEVEN

HAD I believed in hell before, in purgatory? Had I believed in an afterlife in which my smashed body might go on suffering?

There it was, believe it or not, and those potent symbols of dismay from which, when they obtruded in my lifetime, I had been so easily able to turn away, now stood before me in undeniable form. Even as I ran from them, I could not tell what form it was they took, but at one moment I thought they were skeletons and, at the next, devils dressed in shining armour and bearing great lights that burnt me where they touched.

The place I was in – but it seemed not to have dimensions! A beetle crushed against a badly folded cloth could have formed a better idea of his surroundings than I, for though it might be said that I was surrounded with streets and buildings of all kinds, they were always *too close*, pressing against my eyes, in fact.

If dimension had gone wrong, that was because my brain had gone wrong. Most of it had not survived the fall. Too much of it had been entirely lost for me even to guess what had been there before, but I was filled with a desire – no, a mania would be a better word, a mania to establish what the world had been like that I had left. I could recall nothing about that world, except that it was unlike the one I found myself in.

This mania tortured me. What had the world been? What was the world? And what had I been, what manner of being? What was the essential "I" – why had I never ascertained that when I had the chance?

The mania propelled me down a street. More accurate: the mania brought me into a sort of being a street that flowed past me. I flung up my hands to let it slip under my arms.

There were beings on the street, beings much like me. There was also a rigid etiquette that forbade my speaking to certain people, however desperately I needed help, however close I might be to – but in the old world (that I did remember, piercingly sharp!) we had death to drive us; here there was only mania....

I try to put it down calmly, clearly. Of course it won't go. Some foods you can't digest, only spit out. Some poisons don't kill ; they embalm you in a living mummification, where the mind glazes over and becomes a distorting mirror.

Out and out the street rolled. It rattled off a round building that spun like a great drum releasing ribbon – but all the while it was my arms that did it. I understood then, though I don't now. At last the mania drove me to a man who sat over a small fire in the street so that his face was obscured by smoke. The etiquette allowed me to speak to him before he went by because his eyes were hidden.

As we were carried along by the street, I called to him:

"What was the world like that I left? I must know to be set free."

He said: "You do not know about the sheep and the goats then? I can tell you only about the sheep. You must find another who will tell you about the goats."

All this I could hardly understand, for we seemed to be moving along at a grinding rate. Perhaps at this point I was hitting him, but I never saw his face for smoke, and without waiting for an answer, he began to tell me about the sheep, in an automatic manner that suggested that throughout the ages he had had to suffer an endless retelling of his tale.

"There was this big field of sheep," he said. "Many of the sheep had lambs, and they were all vacantly happy. They had no sort of worries, financial, matrimonial, moral, or religious, and the grazing was good.

"The only thing that bothered them was the railway. Running along the side of the field where they preferred to lie was an embankment, along the top of which diesel trains ran.

"Every day, twelve diesel trains ran along the top of the embankment. They never stopped, for there was nothing to stop for, and they never sounded their hooters, for there was nothing to sound their hooters for. But they sped by very fast and noisily.

"Every time one of the trains rushed by, the sheep and the lambs were compelled to get up and run away from the embankment to the far side of their field, because they were afraid the trains might catch them. It was always a long while after the train had gone before they could settle down to their grazing again.

"One of the oldest sheep in the field was considerably wiser than the rest. When they had all stampeded across the field for the twelfth time one day, she addressed the rest of the flock.

" 'My friends,' she said, 'I have studied carefully the path that these horrid metal monsters take when they charge through our pasture. I have observed that they never come down from the embankment. We have always prided ourselves, with some justification, that we have run away so fast that the horrid metal monsters could not catch us. But I want you to consider an entirely new theory, based on my observations. Friends, suppose the horrid metal monsters *cannot* come down from the embankment?"

At this, there was some derisive laughter, particularly from the fleet of foot. Undismayed the old sheep continued.

"'Observe what follows if my theory is correct. If the horrid metal monsters cannot come down from the embankment, then they are not chasing us. In fact, my friends, their perceptions may be so alien they are not even aware of us as they clatter by."

"This was so startlingly novel that everyone began bleating at once. As several sheep pointed out, were this hypothesis true, it would imply that the pasture and they themselves were not central to the scheme of things ; which was an intolerable heresy and should be punished. The fleetest lamb contradicted this, saying that people should be free to think what they liked, provided they kept it to themselves. Where the hypothesis was dangerous was that belief in it would clearly mean nobody would bother to run very fast when the horrid metal monsters came, and in no time the flock would become decadent and unable to run at all.

"When they had all had their say, the wise old sheep spoke again.

"'Fortunately, my theory can be tested empirically,' she said. 'In the morning, when the first horrid metal monster comes, we will not run away. We will lie by the embankment, and you will see that the horrid metal monster flashes by without being aware of us.'

"They greeted this proposal with bleats of horror: it was an insult to common sense. But as night fell, such was the enlightenment of the flock, it became apparent that the wise old sheep would have her way, and that in the morning they would co-operate in this dangerous experiment.

"When the wise old sheep perceived this, she began to have qualms. Supposing she were mistaken, and they were all killed by the horrid metal monsters?

"The rest of the flock fell asleep at last, and she decided she must go alone to the top of the embankment and study the enemy territory. If she saw anything to alarm her, she could then call off the experiment.

"To get to the top of the embankment was more difficult than she had expected. There was wire to be negotiated, a steep slope to be climbed, gorse bushes to be pushed through.

The wise old sheep was unused to such exertions. As she gained the top of the embankment, she suffered a heart attack and died.

"The flock woke in the morning and soon observed the hindquarters of the wise old sheep on the top of the embankment. A council was held. It was generally agreed that to honour her memory they must undertake her experiment.

"So when the first horrid metal monster was heard approaching, every one of the sheep sat tight where she was. The horrid metal monster roared down the line, struck the body of the wise old sheep, plunged over the embankment, and killed all the sheep without exception.

This story baffled me. "What happened?" I asked the faceless man.

"The grass grew tall in the field again."

I left him, or I let the road whirl him away. Now the buildings were moving past more rapidly. The effect was not as if I was running forward, for I was being dragged back with them, but at a slower rate than they.

The mania had me savagely again, and impelled me to speak to an old woman who stood with a stick to support her. Her eyes were closed, or it may be that she had lids with no pupils underneath, but in either case, she never looked at me in the time I was before her.

"I understand nothing," I said. "I only know that there is suffering. Why do we suffer, old woman?"

"I will tell you a story," she said. Though we were both whirling away, she spoke softly, so that I could hardly catch her crazy words.

"When the Devil was a child, he was kept well away from all knowledge of the bitter things of the world. Only the happy things were allowed into his presence. Sin, unhappiness, ugliness, illness, age, all were secret from him.

"One day, the Devil escaped from his nanny and climbed over the garden wall. He walked down the road, full of excitement, until he met an old man bent double with age. The Devil stopped and looked at him.

"'Why do you stare at me?' said the old man. 'Anyone would think you had never seen an old man before.'

"The Devil saw that his eyes were dim, his mouth slack, his skin full of wrinkles.

" 'What has happened to you?' he asked.

" 'This is what happens to everyone. It is an incurable disease called time.'

" 'But what have you done to deserve it?'

" 'Nothing. I have got drunk, I have lied occasionally, I have slept with pretty women, I have worked no more than I had to. But those are not bad things. The punishment is greater than the crime, young man.'

" 'When will you get better?' asked the Devil.

"The old man laughed.

" 'There's a funeral coming along the road behind me. Have a look! That's the only way I'll be cured.'

"The Devil waited where he was, and presently the funeral came up. He climbed into a tree by the roadside, and as the procession passed he looked down into the face of the corpse.

"Although the corpse was that of an old man, he did indeed look more peaceful and less tortured than the old man to whom the Devil had spoken. It seemed as if he was cured, as the old man had said. So the Devil followed the procession to a cemetery to see what would happen next.

"He was surprised to see the body put into a hole and buried. He stayed on the spot until everyone had gone, full of a strange sense of things being wrong. He was still sitting there when one of the servants found him and carried him lovingly home.

"Next day, the Devil escaped over the wall again. He wanted to see if the corpse was properly cured.

"Finding a shovel in the cemetery, he began to dig up the grave. Unfortunately, he had forgotten which was the fresh grave and dug up a lot of older ones. In each hole he found terrible things with very alarming faces full of worms. He decided then that anything was better than the cure called death.

"It was on that day the Devil became sick; on that day, too, he decided what he wanted to be when he grew up."

I stared at the vile old woman with her closed eyes. Like all the inhabitants of this purgatory, she was beyond my understanding. "And what did the Devil become when he grew up?" I demanded.

She laughed at me. "Why, a townsman!" she said.

The road whirled me on, or else it was the mania in me

that pursued me. I seemed to fall down it, and to fall at an increasing rate, so that the other beings there twisted past me like people falling down a cliff. It was confusing, but I felt that I was perhaps asking everyone the wrong questions, or else was making the wrong assumptions, and that this was aggravating my rate of fall.

A small girl was falling beside me, a gaunt child with bright copper locks but a face like parched vellum. I shouted to her above the noise: "How can we find if we are fit for the truth?"

When she smiled at me, she had no teeth, and I took her then for an old dwarf who had dyed her hair.

"There's a tale about that," she said. "All about a poor but proud young man who jumped from a hotel window seventeen storeys above the ground. As he was falling, he wondered if his whole life, and the life of almost everyone he knew, was not based upon illusory values. The ground whirled up –"

"Stop! Stop! Don't tell me how the story ends! That is my story! I shall die if you tell me any more. Now I can see that I still have the power to choose my own ending!"

Even as I spoke these words, I roused partly out of this strange bout of madness. The old hag whirled past me, and I realized that what I had taken for a street was nothing of the kind. These verticals, these ventilation cowls, these rails and windows – formed part of the *Trieste Star*. For I was done with Africa, and was sailing fast for home in my own vessel, with all my troubles behind.

Until now, I had not realized that my ship was armoured; I saw that the grey of the street was nothing more than the shielding that covered almost everything, rendering us impervious to anything but a nuclear attack. As I clung to the wheel – we drove through the grey waters at a tremendous pace – it was hard to see our course, so thoroughly were the windows shielded.

When the coast of England loomed up, bells sounded, and the crew began to cheer. I gave her a touch of additional speed; she responded like a woman; and we climbed up a steep launching ramp and ashore without difficulty. Until that minute, I had not realized that I captained an amphibious craft.

In no time, we arrived at the biggest city. It sat on top of its miles-wide platform, with starved land stretching all round it – I saw tiny withered things tending rows and rows of wilting plants before we launched ourselves up on to the platform. Moving more slowly now, I steered the ship down one of the streets.

All the ratings were leaning over the rail, cheering and waving. In my heart too surged an enormous relief that we were back home. But in the streets I saw things that I did not wish to see.

First I saw how the city was constructed. I saw how the serviceways that ran below the base platform had eliminated the need for all the distributive and supply and administrative vehicles that might once have crowded such a street; they were all automated, and ran below ground. All private vehicles, too, had long ago been eliminated in deference to an efficient public transport of bus and tube. As a result the traffic was negligible and the streets were narrow.

On either side of the streets ran the homes of the citizens, the plebs. They were more like barracks than flats. They spread all over the city, were the city, for the city had decentralized itself; divided into districts, no one district took precedence over another. All government and public offices were indistinguishable from the plebeian buildings in which the workers lived. It was only here and there that the brute form of a factory or distributive broke the drab uniformity.

One of the factories we passed, tall and black and windowless, was a soil manufactory, where synthetic micro-organisms were injected into the sand we brought home from Africa's arid coast.

But the people, the people from whom I had sprung! Eagerly I turned to them, to realize for the first time how brutalized they had become. More and more the faculties of the city were being taken over by machines, and more and more the people were looking like machines. A starved body shows its joints and tendons and stanchions in a manner hardly distinguishable from an ordinary robot.

But robots do not break out with those awful skin diseases. Robots do not develop stomachs and legs distended by beri beri. They never have running sores or scurvy. Their spines do not curve, nor their knees buckle, with rickets. They are unable to walk with a hang-dog look. Their fabrics do not atrophy or their hearts break. I had forgotten, I had forgotten!

Many of these tragic people carried charms with which to ward off illness. Most of them had developed weird cults and religions. Among the more simple-minded, orgies formed a vital if occasional part of their lives ; the shedding of seed was strongly linked with the vital fertility of the soil from which they were for ever cut off. Among the *élite* – for every ant hill has its aristocrats – was an austere cult that forbade sexual intercourse on the grounds that already the world groaned under too many people ; "Let the Earth bring forth a decrease!" was its legend.

All this I saw: and I wept, so that I gave up the wheel, and another of the crew stood by my shoulder and took it. He steered a wilder course than I. He sailed us to city after city, not only in England ; we moved up to Scotland, and then across to the lands of Scandinavia, down to Europe, across the wilds of Russia, over to China, over to America. City after city poured beneath our keel like cobbles under a fleet foot, and each city in its misery and lack of distinction could hardly be told from the next. In all of them the people, the endless people, starved and died and hoped and starved. It was as if that anxious jerking of the loins by which they begot duplicates of themselves was a part of a universal death agony.

"Enough!" I cried.

At once the cities vanished, and were replaced by the sea, the sea at night, a dark and gently breathing expanse of water, grumbling in its bed. Full of relief, I turned to the dark figure at the wheel. It was the *doppelgänger*, the Figure!

Our eyes met. It had eyes if not face – and yet it had face, for I saw for the first time that it was myself, a reflection of myself trapped as it might be in a pool of oil, imprisoned behind some terrible surface of guilt.

Its suffering – this I knew in that first glance when our gazes locked – was inseparable from mine, its damnation was mine, and as it was a lost spirit so was my spirit. Yet for this I felt no compassion, only hate. I leapt at the foul thing.

Even as I seized it by the throat, so it seized me, fighting back savagely. In those anguished seconds, it looked nothing like me. Its fangs gleamed in my face, and I wrestled so that it would not bite off my lips. Now I had a better grip, and tightened it, and tightened it, until I felt the seams of my robe rip. It fought back, clinging to me so that a bloody cloud settled before my eyes and would not shake away. Yet I kept that crazed grip on him, and gradually the light died from his eyes. I gave him a final shake, and we fell together into the pool of oily water.

His figure, his dread face, was below me. Slowly it slid down, away from the surface. One hand came up as the rest sank; its fingers touched my fingers, then it all was lost in the rippling dark of the sea.

I still stood looking, long after what had seemed my reflection had shrunk and gone from the water. Our most profound moments come in such periods of inactivity. From the ocean of myself, I knew something had evaporated. Almost for the first time, I was conscious of the way in which my life had been dogged by illness and delusion. What sort of phantom the Figure was, I still could not say; perhaps it has been my mind's projection of a wish to escape from my own wretched circumstances, its best endeavour to create the free being I was not. However that might be, I realized that it was gone now; peace stole over me like a rising tide, as I understood that I should never again hand over the wheel to it.

Philosophy is not my strong point, though I have tried many a time to make sense of my life, and of the killing drag of history, but I tried then to review the phantasies that my sickness had inflicted on me. Some I have set down in this narrative. At the time, they held as firm a place in my understanding as parts of the real world, and the continents of delusion through which I had been forced to march were no more fantastic than Africa or England.

But the ocean that linked all continents forced itself on to my attention. Slopping round my body, it reminded me that I was cold and had better crawl out of it.

The mere thought of the effort made me feel terribly ill. Darkness whirled inside and outside my head.

I trod water, gasping. Slowly, a different sort of awareness came back to me. The pounding in my head seemed to bring it back. I caught a smell of onions frying, and flowers, but so faint ... and then lost in my bursting head. So intense was

111

the migraine for some while that I could not look out of my eyes to find where I was. At last the cloud lifted. I looked about me. There lay the half-finished, half-ruinous city of Walvis Bay. I was staring at it through the dark of night and from a strange angle; I stood up to my chest in the sea, under a pier that jutted out from the main promenade. I was back in my right mind at last, and someone was stalking me nearby.

CHAPTER TWELVE

I MADE no attempt to evade whoever was after me. My will was directed to wading ashore, so that the low swells rolling up the beach did not bowl me off my feet and drown me.

The pillars of the pier were encrusted with seaweed. I leant against them with the water swilling round my ankles, trying to reorient myself. Although I was tired, I felt extraordinarily well, now that my head stopped pounding – had I not conquered my own personal devil? But what did that mean, how had it improved me, morally, spiritually, physically? As yet I could not tell, unless the lack of fear I felt for the man lurking in the shadows was a portent.

The last thing I recalled of the external world was my plunge to the ground with the anit-gravity unit. That I lived was proof that it had carried me safely down to the street. But what had that cathartic plunge done to me, and could it have had some tonic effect on my nerves and glands to the extent that the scintillating scotoma with which I was afflicted was at last cured? Again, I could not tell; but the uncharacteristic quality of my recent delusions, and their intensity, led me to hope so.

Of course I wondered what I had been doing during the hours that obviously had elapsed since I jumped from the hotel window. I had escaped detection by Peter Mercator's forces – that was clear; nothing else was. What was Justine doing now, where was Thunderpeck?

But I was weary of questions.

I looked towards the promenade, where strings of bright lights burned. Music was playing, and I saw numerous people in silhouette, shadows within shadows, walking along the front. Walvis Bay was filling up for the President's opening ceremony. I could also see the outline of the man who watched me, dimly lit as he stood on the beach and half-concealed by the supports of the pier.

Something was wedged in the angle of the uprights against which I rested. It had been stuck where it was for some while, for the action of the sea had worn most of it smooth and barnacles clung to it. When I pulled it free, it proved to be a length of a thin beam, with an iron bolt in one end; perhaps it had once formed part of a native boat, lost along the coast; in any case, it made a useful if cumbersome weapon. Concealing my movements, I tucked it into the top of my trousers under the bedraggled robe I wore.

"What do you want with me?" I called.

The outline at once stood away from the pier, with no attempt at camouflage.

"Are you in your right mind at last?" he asked. I knew the voice.

"Is that you, Mercator? We'd better have a talk."

"That's what I've been hoping for."

I waded heavily out of the water. Mercator was no longer a figure of fear to me; it behoved me to discover what I could from him.

So we met on the beach, with the ocean grumbling behind us. When we had stared at each other long enough in the pale illumination cast by the lights on the distant promenade, we sat down facing one another. His face looked lined and ghastly, and I felt mine was too.

"How long have you been following me?"

"Not for very long, although I have been looking for you for several hours – ever since you hit me on the jaw and left the hotel with more ingenuity than sense." His voice was husky; I could hardly hear him above the noise of the surf breaking.

"I did not disappear effectively enough."

"Certainly you didn't. When you jumped out of the window in that foolhardy way, you landed in a side street and then began to walk about openly, peering into people's faces and talking to yourself. Israt and I would certainly have caught you again, had we not had other troubles."

"What other troubles?" The sand was sticky and unpleasant between my hands as I sat there.

"We are being watched. Everyone is against everyone else here. They are particularly suspicious of a foreigner like me with an acquaintance like you. You know the anit-grav unit you borrowed? It belonged to the Prime Minister of Algeria, General Ramayanner Kurdan. Old Kurdan makes a dangerous enemy. Algeria's history over the past two or three hundred –"

"Never mind their history, Mercator. Of course they will be against you, if you plan to assassinate the President of Africa tomorrow. I am against it, and heaven knows I'm politically uncommitted. Isn't el Mahasset generally known as the most capable statesman Africa has ever thrown up, a mixture of Nehru, Chou En-lai, and Churchill?"

"Yes, yes, Noland, I agree with you, but you see that's just the point –" He stopped suddenly and clutched his chest. He sagged forward, until his brow almost touched the sand. When he pulled his torso upright again, his face was harsh and strained, and his voice when he spoke was shaky. "You're by no means the only sick man on the beach. Crisis – I came away without my pills. Do you realize that the ideal of health is gone from the world? It's patriotic to be sick nowadays."

"Look, Mercator, I don't need your lecture. I'm sorry if you're ill now but I want nothing to do with you. I never intended to get involved with your affairs in the first place."

"Don't talk like that, Knowle. You are involved, and you know it. This issue concerns you and everyone." The spasm was over now and he pulled himself together. "Listen, I followed you patiently because I have to ask you to do something."

"Where's your pet thug, Israt?"

He let anger ride into his voice. "Israt overcame your Doctor Thunderpeck and joined me, but got separated from me in the crowds in the streets. I just hope he is safe. In any case, he is not my pet thug; we happen to belong to the same religion – we are both Abstainers. Neither of us have done you any harm."

"Ha! What about those wretched years I spent on your wretched farm?"

"Oh, use a little sense. Forget about that! Besides, I was only nominally in control of the farm. You can see how throughout the last centuries farmers have slowly become divorced from their land. It was inevitable when the farms, under pressure from so-called efficiency, grew larger and larger. When I retired this year, I was nothing more then a man who handled vast amounts of records and paperwork; I was as much shackled to my job as you were to yours."

"You should try a few years in one of your stinking villages before you say that."

"I am not responsible for the punitive system, Noland. I had no say in who worked the land. I am not trying to exonerate myself from blame, and certainly I am not trying to defend a system I in fact found more offensive than you did." He dug his fingers into the sand and I saw that he was in pain again. "Listen, Noland, for God's sake! I want your help, I beg you to help, before it is too late."

"Sorry, no. Now let's get you back to your doctor."

"That can wait. Listen, I must trust you – not so much because you are a fellow countryman as because I can trust no African on an emotional topic such as this."

"You're mad, Mercator. Come on, let me get you back to the hotel." As I bent to try and pick him up, he was protesting all the while, but I cut him off. "I ought to hand you over to the police – I would if I did not want to get involved. This idea you have of shooting el Mahasset is pure craziness."

He was resisting my attempts to lift him. "It's about that I have to speak to you. Noland, I know you're pretty tough and unscrupulous. I want you to shoot el Mahasset for me. Believe me, I'll make it worth your while."

In sheer surprise, I let go of him. He pulled himself up on to his knees, coughing and clutching himself.

"Mahasset's got to go! We don't want Africa united. With the President out of the way, the African states will fall apart. They will war with each other, and their allies in America and Europe will be drawn in. It will result in nuclear war on the largest possible scale. The whole current structure of society will be wiped out." He faltered and said: "Noland, I'm sick. It's a cancerous growth in my lungs. . . . But you hear what I'm saying. I can't rely any more on myself to shoot the President. You must do it."

I dropped on my knees beside him, clenching my fist at him.

"You think I'd help you plunge the world into war? You're crazy, Mercator! I'd have known that right from the start if I'd bothered to look properly at the hints dropped in those letters Justine wrote you. Who's got those letters anyhow?"

"I've got them, here, but I beg you to listen to my argument –"

"I've heard enough," I said. "Believe me, Mercator, I'm sorry for you. But I'm not going to shoot the President. Nor are you. Nobody is. Perhaps you're nothing worse than a crazy idealist, but it's idealists who've been causing trouble in the world for thousands of years."

His face was distorted. "Spare me your speculations, you stupid pleb!"

I stood up. "I'll go and get your doctor to you, Mercator, and then I'm informing the police of where you are and what you are planning."

I climbed up on to the promenade, trailing sand and water from my garments.

He called to me until I was lost among the people on the front and could no longer hear.

The crowds were thinning now. As I passed the top of the great President's Square, the completed buildings of which were illuminated by floodlight, I saw by the clock on the highest tower that the time was past midnight. This was already the day of the President's arrival.

As I walked, I became less conscious of weariness than of a curious lightness in me which I associated with hunger. I seemed beyond the craving for food but badly needed a drink. So I steered my thoughts from myself and tried to evaluate what Mercator had told me. Why should a man, even a madman, want to destroy the world? I recalled what he had said earlier about having invested in anti-gravity research. Putting the two conversations together, I thought I had the answer ; he would engineer a war so that he could become bigger and richer. Under its present grinding poverty, with most of its technological efforts devoted to agriculture and allied technologies, the world was only slowly developing anit-gravity as a commercial proposition. But a war would accelerate that development wonderfully ; and Mercator, sick as he

116

was, could not afford to wait to reap the rewards of his foresight.

So I diagnosed the situation, and horrified myself by it.

For all that, I stuck to my word to go first to the South Atlantic Hotel to fetch the man's doctor. So much I would do, if only for Justine's sake.

Although the door to the Mercator suite was ajar, I had no premonition of ill as I went in. But when I entered the living-room, it was to be confronted by chaos. I could see at once that the place had been hastily searched. Contents of drawers and cupboards had been tipped on to the floor, vases broken, pictures set awry or smashed, tables overturned. Even the carpet had been dragged from the floor and flung into one corner. Sprawled over the back of an armchair lay Israt. I ran to him, calling his name, but he was dead.

A dagger with a beautifully wrought silver handle stuck from his gown ; he had been stabbed through the back. By the signs, I saw that he had been stabbed five or more times, and I wondered how anyone could contain that much vengefulness.

Some warmth was still left in his body. This murder had not long been committed. As I stood there dazed, wondering what had become of the lovely and fateful Justine, I heard a sound from the next room. With a chill taking me, I thought that perhaps the murderer still lurked there. As I backed away from the bedroom door, it opened slowly. Mercator's doctor was there, crawling forward on his hands and knees.

I went over and helped the little man to his feet. His face was absolutely bloodless, and I felt mine to be the same. His restless hands, which I had noted before, trembled round his body as if seeking a way of escape. I poured us both a drink of brandy from a bottle that had fallen from the ransacked cocktail cabinet without breaking. After that we felt better.

"It was terrible!" the doctor said, lighting a mescahale. "He breathed like an animal! I'll swear he knew I was hiding in there, in the bedroom, under the bed, but after he had killed Israt – he growled over it! – he seemed to have had enough. I didn't hear him leave. I just lay there in a sort of paralysis until you came along."

"Who was this killer?"

"I don't know his name. But he screamed to Israt as he killed him something about a friend of Israt's stealing his Prime Minister's anti-grav unit. Was that you?

"I stole an anti-grav unit, yes, but you're not laying this murder at my door. This whole concern is nothing to do with me."

"So I've heard you say before, and each time I believe you less. Mind if I just sit down? My legs are still shaking. The – the murderer made such a noise, you know. Anyhow, this Algerian also said that he knew Israt was Mercator's tool, and he thought that Mercator was plotting with New Angola against Algeria. That was why he killed Israt, on instructions from his boss."

I'd finished the brandy, and my mind was beginning to work again. I stopped listening to the doctor's ramblings. I saw that many people were threatened in this situation, including people of whom I was fond. It was necessary that I joined forces with Justine and Thunderpeck as soon as possible.

When I questioned him, the old doctor could tell me nothing of either Justine or Thunderpeck. So I told him where Mercator was, and said he had better go and tend him. It came to me that I knew where to find Thunderpeck, if he was still alive, for we had agreed on a rendezvous. And directly the doctor had left, I would phone through the Walvis Bay police and tell them to pick up Mercator before his crazy assassination plan got any further – without, of course, giving my name.

"You look all in," the doctor said. "Before I go to Mercator, let me give you a pill to keep you on your feet. Will you still be here when Mr. Mercator and I get back?"

"You worry about him, I'll look after myself."

"I am worrying about him, Mr. Noland. He's a very sick man, and all this running about may kill him. But that's no reason why I can't help you."

I took the pill he gave me and swallowed it automatically, as I have been swallowing pills every day of my life. As he left, I turned into the bathroom to get myself a drink of water. It tasted wonderful, rusty though it was! I drank a couple of tumblers full, and as the last drop went down, I clutched hold of the towel rail to steady myself, staggered, and slid to the floor, out to the wide.

It was an elementary mistake to make, to forget that the little doctor was an ally of the madman who was out to wreck the peace of the world. . . .

CHAPTER THIRTEEN

DAWN came in like an albatross from the antipodes of the world, brushed me with its wings and woke me. I pushed the towels away and sat up, wondering what I could possibly be doing on a bathroom floor. That would have been an ideal night for hallucinations and the devils that visit by night, yet I had slept deeply and serenely, and awoke feeling in good health. Being starvingly hungry merely set an edge to my health.

Facts came clicking back into place. This was the day Mercator planned to slay the President of Africa. Mercator was a villain in a hotel full of villains – a hotel where I had slept unmolested! I remembered the dead thing in the next room, and how it looked. I remembered that I must hunt for old Thunderpeck and the strange and fatal Justine Smith.

Well, there was no time like the present!

I tried to collect another glass of water to moisten my dry mouth, but the taps this morning ran so slowly that I gave up. Now that I was moving, anxiety tugged at me.

With the idea of looking less conspicuous, I put on a clean robe of Mercator's. Trying not to think what I was doing, I removed the silver-hilted dagger from Israt's rib cage, cleaned it on his gown, and held it up my sleeve. It might be needed; there was no telling who kept a watch on Mercator's room.

Suddenly it struck me that Mercator should have been back with the doctor long before this. Something had gone wrong there – to my advantage.

I left the suite more cautiously than I had entered. No one was about. On the ground floor, only servants moved with the slow-motion surliness that is their prerogative at that time of day.

This was the cool and transitory hour when the sun is risen and has yet to take command of its domain ; this is the spring that comes every day with its cool airs to the tropics. I love it, and took delight in it even then, when my heart laboured with anxiety.

Thunderpeck and I had arranged to meet at the foot of the tallest tower in the President's Square. But how long would he wait? I knew nothing of his movements since Israt overpowered him during the previous afternoon.

To my surprise, the streets were already busy. Builders' lorries had been pressed into service and slowly toured the streets, piled high with the flags of African nations. Men with tall ladders climbed lamp-posts, stringing up pennants and bunting. In President's Square, it was the same story, and the same activity reigned. Here a large dais had been assembled in the centre of the square, and from a van labelled "All Africa Radio", electricians were unloading television cameras and microphones. A generator stood nearby, cables from it snaking across unfinished mosaic work.

Police were also active, and I took care to avoid them as I came to the high tower of the temple. When I found there was no sign of Thunderpeck at all, I realized I had hardly been expecting any. For a while I stood waiting, listening to the distant sound of the surf as it rolled against the beach after its long ride East to find Africa. Then I slipped inside the temple.

As far as I could remember it, Thunderpeck and I had agreed to meet at the foot of the tower. He might very well have interpreted this literally ; certainly inside would be a safer place to wait.

Inside the temple, lamps of an ornate pattern burned, suspended at intervals from chains hanging from the distant roof. In here, darkness still ruled, and the light from the windows wore a muffled stealthy look. The air held a heavy sweetness. I did not go into the main body of the temple, where barely glimpsed figures prostrated themselves on the bare floor, praying for grace to confront a new day. Instead, I turned behind a sandalwood screen, and passed through a small room – a robing room? – in search of the foot of the tower.

As I went, I was aware of a man's voice, singing in a side chamber of the temple. He chanted, and the chant was accompanied on a droning instrument like an Indian tamboura ; the sound took me by the throat, so that I almost stopped to listen. It reminded me that there were realms whose very ground-plan I was unable to comprehend.

Through the robing-room was the base of the tower proper. Here it was exceedingly dark, since a curtain cut it off from the light in the robing-room, and only a faint illumination filtered down from the belfry far over my head. Apprehensively, I called in almost a whisper: "Thunderpeck?"

As my eyes grew accustomed to the light, I saw there was no way of ascending to the top of the tower except by electric lift, and that the cage rested at ground level.

I called again. Whas there some faint movement far above me, where the morning was?

Still uneasy, I wondered if I should wait here. There was no place of concealment, except for the narrow space behind the lift. As I went to investigate it, my eye fell on something bundled into the narrow space. It was a man, bent double and enveloped in an Arab burnous. Sickness rose in my gullet even before I had pulled him out and recognized my old friend and doctor. His throat was cut.

As I looked down at Thunderpeck's elaborately acned face, grief welled up in me.

Much good waiting here for me had done him! I guessed that once again the Algerian assassin had been active.

The voice of the singer climbed up to the highest reaches of the temple. It was a chant full of longing for peace and an end to loneliness. Hearing it, I wept. I buried my face in my hands and let the long sobs rack me.

Even as I wept, as I could not have done a while before, even as I was riven by the fact of Thunderpeck's death, I felt myself whole. I had wanted to tell him about my last encounter with the Figure to see what he made of it; now I should never hear him say: "It was a symptom of your schizophrenia, and now it is over and you are at peace with yourself again." I vowed as I wept that I would do better in future.

It was the noise from the lift shaft that brought me back to the world. I wiped my eyes, proud that I had cried. If Thunderpeck's murderer were still here, he should have as good as he gave! I looked up the shaft, and down to me came my own name, hollow and strange in the confining tower: "Knowle!"

Justine was up there!

The thought crossed my mind that it might be she who had – but no, there were signs that the doctor, whose body was already frozen with rigor mortis, had put up a fight with his assailant ; so this could be no crime of my fine and fatal Justine's!

I climbed into the lift cage. It was a tiny affair that would contain no more than two men at a time. It drew me up almost in silence, and through the occasional narrow window I saw daylight, and splinters of Walvis Bay, and the sea, and the confused world. Then the top was gained, and as I opened the door, Justine came into my arms.

At any other time, what joy that would have brought me! Her dark hair was against my cheek, her body warm and soft against mine. How long we stood like that I cannot tell, but eventually she drew back and looked at me.

"So Peter sent you!" she exclaimed. "Thank goodness he sent someone – I have no head for heights. You're only just in time. It's now quarter to eight."

"In time for what?"

"At eight, the security men will cordon off President's Square, and after that only invited guests will be able to enter."

"How long have you been here, Justine?" I was staring at her face, hungrily, viewing again the pale countenance that had such unreasonable power over me.

"I got here shortly after six, while it was still dark. I have been awake half the night waiting for Peter to phone me ; when he didn't, I knew I had to come up here myself and do the job."

"Justine, I don't understand. What job are you talking about?"

"Really, Knowle, what do you think? The President appears with his retinue in the square at ten o'clock. When he stands up to make his speech, that's when we shoot him."

We sent the lift cage down to the bottom of its shaft. I followed her up a short wooden flight of steps to a platform over which hung one single black wide-mouthed bell. I saw that she had spread a rug here for herself, and had brought also a cushion and a vacuum flask and a high-powered repeating rifle with telescopic sights. It lay across the rug.

She put her hand through my arm.

"You'll be all right, Knowle? I mean, you're a good shot? You can do it? We must make no mistakes."

"Look, Justine – Justine, you're mad, or you're hypnotized by Mercator, who is as crazy as you. You know as well as I do that President el Mahasset is a good man, that he's the only man that can keep Africa and the world at peace. We can't shoot him! You care nothing for me; you care for Mercator, your beloved Peter. That being so, you must know why he wants the President shot."

She stood back and regarded me, her head tilted slightly upwards so that I could see the beautiful column of her neck. She had a narrow white rim to the collar of her dress; otherwise she was unrelievedly in black – perhaps in the dress she had mentioned in one of her letters. Even her eyes were dark as she stared at me, and I thought what a fine picture of an executioner she made. Her face was hard as she said: "Tell me why Peter wants the President killed, Knowle."

So I explained about Mercator's money being now invested in anti-gravity research and about the way I calculated he could profit from a global war. As I talked, she turned away, in a gesture of weariness and disgust. Without being able to stop it, I heard my voice tail lamely away.

"What a filthy materialist argument you produce!" she said quietly.

"No, Justine. Don't try and dodge the truth by calling it names. You must forget this assassination business. I have reason to think that Mercator is dead by now, killed along with his doctor by his enemies, or he would have returned to the hotel before I left. Forget him and forget all this nonsense, and leave here at once with me."

"You'll never move me!"

"You've got to get out before the police reach us. Your letters were in Mercator's pocket and by now you will be incriminated."

As if she had not heard me, she turned to face me and said again: "What a filthy materialist argument you use to dirty Peter's motives! Knowle, just for once let me tell you the truth for you to hear. Just see if you can take it! From the start, you have misjudged Peter and me. He was a farmer and you feared him. Yet he worked constantly to mitigate conditions on the land – even those beyond his control. He helped

123

you, though you never had the grace to acknowledge it. Now he is working for a common good, but it is so far above your head that you will never understand it. In the same way, I feel you have never understood me – not that that matters.

"Let me show you how mistaken you have been and are. Both Peter and I belong to one of the numerous secret religions that proliferate throughout the miserable cities of the world. But ours, the cult of Abstinence, is the strictest of all. Have you heard of the Abstainers?"

I had, but I thought it was only a fad that entertained some members of the upper echelons of society.

"The Abstainers," Justine said, "do all in their power to get the mass of people to use proper methods of birth control ; yet although some of these methods have been in existence for centuries, you cannot force them successfully on a population that has sunk below a certain level of social awareness."

"Who caused it to sink?" I asked hotly. "You forget that I can read, Justine! I'm not the fool you take me for. I've studied history books. I know the poor people were once a darn sight better off than we are now."

Despairingly, she said: "History is not only confined to books. It's the medium in which we live. It is true that the poor were once better off, but they have sunk under their own weight! The farmers know that the way they have to exploit the land to feed the great greedy mass is wrong, but what else can they do? What does the average moron care for the law of diminishing returns? The demand is for quantity. The farmers have to meet that demand or they themselves are imprisoned. Land conservation just doesn't make economic sense when there are twenty-four thousand million people in the world."

"You've learnt your lesson well! Have you done?" I spoke sullenly. There were pains in my belly.

"No, I've not done. I was telling you about the Abstainers. We have vowed to abstain from sexual intercourse, and –"

"That's impossible!"

"We have proved it is possible, and so have others before us. To your kind, loving may have no more significance than a glass of hooch. To us it is deeply significant, and a thing of deep disgust, for from it comes the propagation of the human species, and that is already enough out of hand."

At that, I could not help laughing. "Much good a handful of you can do!"

"But we can! We can kill the President, we can start a world war! It's the only way to break the awful cycle that has become established. Try to understand, Knowle, please. The *status quo* must be thrown on to its ear. Human life is no longer sacred – we are at a period of history where it is a blasphemy, love-making a perversion! The whole world situation is a tragedy!

"Think of the cities, Knowle – you lived in them most of your life, think of the degraded rabble that inhabits them, divorced from the earth and from any natural and lovely thing, slaves to ignorance and superstition and illness. Examine your own unhappy life! Think of what it is like to labour on the land. Once it was a good thing! Now – you know this – you have to cross the earth as if you crossed the face of Mars ; you have to be branded a criminal before you can be directed to go there. Shouldn't a system that has brought such things about go toppling into the dust?"

We stood staring at each other, both brought to silence. I cannot tell what I thought, only that I trembled. There I stood, and she poured me coffee from her vacuum flask and brought it to me. Still I stood there.

"Think of the misery of your own life, the guilt and sickness and mistrust, and how it should never have been so," she said. Her tone was only compassionate. When I did not answer, she did not press me.

Absent, I drank the coffee. At last I said: "But if this war comes, who's to survive?"

She gave me then a gentle look, and for the first time I knew I was in the presence of the woman who had written the love letters.

"The people best equipped to survive," she answered, "will survive. I mean the only people who even in these grim past years have had the courage to live their independent lives – the Travellers. You know something of them, I believe."

"I do."

She sat down. Slowly I sank beside her. She laid a hand on my knee, where it remained limply as if it had passed on a burden too great for it.

"We're not really assassins, Knowle," she said. "We're

midwives. A new way of living has got to come, and the sooner the old one goes the better."

As she handed me the rifle, I could hear the sound below us of many people assembling in the square. Inside the temple, untroubled by the terrors of the world, the voices of the faithful rose and fell. Ignoring the rumbling of my empty stomach, I cradled the rifle under one arm and crawled towards the nearest window slit.

Science Fiction and Fantasy from Methuen Paperbacks

While every effort is made to keep prices low, it is sometimes necessary to increase prices at short notice. Methuen Paperbacks reserves the right to show new retail prices on covers which may differ from those previously advertised in the text or elsewhere.

The prices shown below were correct at the time of going to press.

☐	413 55450 3	**Half-Past Human**	T J Bass	£1.95
☐	413 58160 8	**Rod of Light**	Barrington J Bayley	£2.50
☐	417 04130 6	**Colony**	Ben Bova	£2.50
☐	413 57910 7	**Orion**	Ben Bova	£2.95
☐	417 07280 5	**Voyagers**	Ben Bova	£1.95
☐	417 06760 7	**Hawk of May**	Gillian Bradshaw	£1.95
☐	413 56290 5	**Chronicles of Morgaine**	C J Cherryh	£2.95
☐	413 51310 6	**Downbelow Station**	C J Cherryh	£1.95
☐	413 51350 5	**Little Big**	John Crowley	£3.95
☐	417 06200 1	**The Golden Man**	Philip K Dick	£1.75
☐	413 58860 2	**Wasp**	Eric Frank Russell	£2.50
☐	413 59770 9	**The Alchemical Marriage of Alistair Crompton**	Robert Sheckley	£2.25
☐	413 41920 7	**Eclipse**	John Shirley	£2.50
☐	413 59990 6	**All Flesh is Grass**	Clifford D Simak	£2.50
☐	413 58800 9	**A Heritage of Stars**	Clifford D Simak	£2.50
☐	413 55590 9	**The Werewolf Principle**	Clifford D Simak	£1.95
☐	413 58640 5	**Where the Evil Dwells**	Clifford D Simak	£2.50
☐	413 54600 4	**Raven of Destiny**	Peter Tremayne	£1.95
☐	413 56840 7	**This Immortal**	Roger Zelazny	£1.95
☐	413 56850 4	**The Dream Master**	Roger Zelazny	£1.95
☐	413 41550 3	**Isle of the Dead**	Roger Zelazny	£2.50

All these books are available at your bookshop or newsagent, or can be ordered direct from the publisher. Just tick the titles you want and fill in the form below.

Methuen Paperbacks, Cash Sales Department,
PO Box 11, Falmouth,
Cornwall TR10 109EN.

Please send cheque or postal order, no currency, for purchase price quoted and allow the following for postage and packing:

UK	60p for the first book, 25p for the second book and 15p for each additional book ordered to a maximum charge of £1.90.
BFPO and Eire	60p for the first book, 25p for the second book and 15p for each next seven books, thereafter 9p per book.
Overseas Customers	£1.25 for the first book, 75p for the second book and 28p for each subsequent title ordered.

NAME (Block Letters) ....

ADDRESS..

....